"Let me hold my son," he urged, with unconcealed impatience

Elinor did not want to risk a scene that might upset her child. She handed Sami over. Jasim clasped the little boy with care and held him out to examine him, keenly scrutinizing every inch of Sami's fearless little face. There was a quality of bemusement and wonder in Jasim's stern gaze that unsettled Elinor and made her feel very uncomfortable. Brown eyes sparkling, Sami smiled at Jasim and made no objection when Jasim brought him closer. His father's confident handling made it clear that he was no stranger to young children.

"He is the only boy born in my family for many years," Jasim said gravely. "It is a crime that we have been unable to celebrate his birth."

A...*crime*? Well, that more than hinted at the weight of blame he intended to foist on her. Resentment stirred like a knife twisting inside her, and her soft mouth compressed into a mutinous line. "If Sami weren't present, I would tell you exactly how I fe

Jasim elevated a
was astonished
I am interested
walked out on o

**Bestselling Harlequin Presents author,
Lynne Graham is back with a
fabulous new trilogy!**

Three ordinary girls—a little bit naive,
but also honest and plucky…

Three fabulously wealthy, impossibly handsome
and very ruthless men…

When opposites attract and passion leads
to pregnancy…it can only mean marriage!

Pregnant Brides

*Inexperienced and expecting,
they're forced to marry!*

Coming Next Month
Ruthless Magnate, Convenient Wife
Sergei and Alissa's story

Coming in March
Greek Tycoon, Inexperienced Mistress
Atreus and Lindy's story

Lynne Graham

DESERT PRINCE, BRIDE OF INNOCENCE

PREGNANT BRIDES

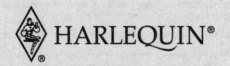

TORONTO • NEW YORK • LONDON
AMSTERDAM • PARIS • SYDNEY • HAMBURG
STOCKHOLM • ATHENS • TOKYO • MILAN • MADRID
PRAGUE • WARSAW • BUDAPEST • AUCKLAND

Recycling programs
for this product may
not exist in your area.

ISBN-13: 978-0-373-12884-6

DESERT PRINCE, BRIDE OF INNOCENCE

First North American Publication 2010.

Copyright © 2009 by Lynne Graham.

www.eHarlequin.com

Printed in U.S.A.

All about the author…
Lynne Graham

Born of Irish/Scottish parentage, **LYNNE GRAHAM**
has lived in Northern Ireland all her life. She has one
brother. She grew up in a seaside village and now lives
in a country house surrounded by a woodland garden,
which is wonderfully private.

Lynne first met her husband when she was fourteen.
They married after she completed a degree at
Edinburgh University. Lynne wrote her first book at
fifteen and it was rejected everywhere. She started
writing again when she was at home with her first
child. It took several attempts before she sold her first
book, and the delight of seeing that first book for sale in
the local newsagents has never been forgotten.

Lynne always wanted a large family, and she has five
children. Her eldest and her only natural child is in her
twenties and a university graduate. Her other children,
who are every bit as dear to her heart, are adopted:
two from Sri Lanka and two from Guatemala. In Lynne's
home, there is a rich and diverse cultural mix, which
adds a whole extra dimension of interest and discovery
to family life.

The family has two pets. Thomas, a very large and
affectionate black cat, bosses the dog and hunts rabbits.
The dog is Daisy, an adorable but not very bright white
West Highland white terrier, who loves being chased by
the cat. At night, dog and cat sleep together in front of
the kitchen stove.

Lynne loves gardening and cooking, collects everything
from old toys to rock specimens and is crazy about
every aspect of Christmas.

CHAPTER ONE

His royal highness, Prince Jasim bin Hamid al Rais, frowned when his aide told him that his brother's wife was waiting to see him. 'You should have told me that the Princess was here. My family always have first call on my time,' he admonished.

Jasim was renowned in financial circles for the astute speed and strategy he utilised in the pursuit of profit in the Rais international business empire, and his employees had a healthy respect for their chairman. He was a tough employer who set high standards and accepted nothing less than excellence. His natural survival skills were honed to a fine cutting edge by a challenging family and palace politics. He was a tall, powerfully built man in his early thirties and he was possessed of a degree of dark, devastating good looks and potent masculinity that women found irresistible.

His French-born sister-in-law, Yaminah, was a small, rather homely brunette with a strained set to her rounded face that warned him that she was struggling to control her emotions. Jasim greeted the older woman with warmth and concern. To see her he was keeping a government minister waiting, but his smooth sophistication was more than equal to the task of hiding that fact and he ordered refreshments and asked her to sit down as if time were of no object.

'Are you comfortable at Woodrow Court?' His elder brother, Crown Prince Murad, and his family were currently using Jasim's country house in Kent while they had a brand new English property built to order nearby.

'Oh, yes. It's a wonderful house and we are being very well looked after,' Yaminah rushed to assure him. 'But we never meant to put you out of your own home, Jasim. Won't you come down this weekend?'

'Of course, if you would like me to but, believe me, I am very comfortable in my town house. It is not a sacrifice to stay in the city,' Jasim responded. 'But that is not why you are here to see me, is it? I believe something may be troubling you?'

Yaminah compressed her lips, her anxious brown gaze suddenly flooding with tears. With an exclamation of embarrassment and a choked apology, she drew out a tissue and mopped at her overflowing eyes. 'I shouldn't be bothering you with this, Jasim—'

Jasim sat down in the sofa opposite her in an effort to make the older woman feel more at ease. 'You have never *bothered* me in your life,' he reproved her. 'Why are you worrying about such a thing?'

Yaminah breathed in slow and deep. 'It's…it's our nanny.'

His dark brows drew together in a satiric quirk that questioned her tragic tone of voice. 'If the nanny my staff engaged to take care of my niece is not to your liking, sack her.'

'If only it were so simple…' Yaminah sighed, shredding the tissue between her restless hands and staring down at it. 'She is an excellent nanny and Zahrah is very fond of her. I'm afraid that the problem is…Murad.'

Jasim immediately became very still. His self-discipline was absolute and his lean, strong face betrayed nothing of his exasperation. His brother had always been a womaniser and his lifestyle had got him into trouble more than once. Such a weakness was a dangerous flaw in the future ruler of a small oil-rich and very conservative country like Quaram. Even worse, if Murad was targeting a member of his household right beneath his loyal and loving wife's nose his behaviour had reached a new inexcusable low in his brother's opinion.

'I cannot sack the girl. It would infuriate Murad if I was to interfere. At present I believe it is only a flirtation but she is a *very* beautiful girl, Jasim,' his sister-in-law murmured shakily. 'If she leaves our employ it will only drive the affair out into the open and, you know, Murad really cannot afford to be involved in another scandal.'

'I agree. The King has no patience left with him.' His handsome mouth settling into a grim line, Jasim wondered in angry frustration if his parent's weak heart would even withstand the stress of another upsetting outbreak of bad publicity and scurrilous gossip about his firstborn's morals. Would his elder brother *ever* learn sense and restraint? Why could he never put the needs of his family first? The older man seemed unable to withstand temptation and, this time around, Jasim felt unnervingly responsible. After all, *his* people had hired the wretched nanny! Why hadn't it occurred to him to order an embargo on appointing a young and beautiful woman?

His brother's wife studied him anxiously. 'Will you help me, Jasim?'

Jasim dealt her a wry look. 'Murad will not accept advice from me.'

'He is too stubborn to take advice from anyone, but you *could* help me,' Yaminah told him urgently.

Jasim frowned, believing that she overestimated his influence with his brother. Murad had not been the heir to the throne of Quaram for over fifty years without acquiring a healthy sense of his own importance. While Jasim was very fond of the older man, he knew his brother was equally fond of getting his own way, even if doing so meant trampling on other people. 'In what way might I help?'

Yaminah worried at her lower lip with her teeth. 'If you were prepared to show an interest in her yourself, the problem would disappear,' she declared in a sudden burst of enthusiasm. 'You're young and single and Murad is middle-aged and married. There can be no comparison and the girl is certain to turn her attention to you instead—'

Distaste at such a suggestion slivering through his lean, well-built frame and cooling his eyes to the darkness of a wintry night, Jasim raised his hands in a gesture that urged restraint and calm. 'Yaminah, please be sensible—'

'I am being sensible. Furthermore, if Murad thought you had a fancy for the girl, I'm convinced that he would step back,' Yaminah asserted doggedly. 'He has often said how much he wishes you would meet a woman—'

'But not one on whom *he* has set his heart,' Jasim was moved to insert drily.

'No, you are wrong. Since that…er…unpleasant business with that Englishwoman you were with a few years ago, Murad has been sincerely troubled by the fact that you are still unmarried. He mentioned it only yesterday, and if he believed that *you* were interested in Elinor Tempest he would leave her alone!' the older woman forecast with a vehemence that betrayed how desperate she was to win him round to her state of thinking.

His lean, strong face clenching, Jasim was tense. Indeed his bronzed skin had paled across his hard cheekbones, for the episode in his life that she was referring to was one he preferred not to recall. When the tabloid press had exposed the sleazy past of the woman he had planned to marry three years earlier, Jasim had experienced a degree of rage and humiliation over his own lack of judgement that he was in no way eager to recall. Ever since he had remained resolutely single and he now chose women only to warm his bed and entertain him. Lower expectations had led to much greater satisfaction, he acknowledged inwardly.

Although he had immediately discounted Yaminah's dramatic request for his assistance, however, he remained troubled enough by her visit to want more information about the woman who was the cause of her distress. He instructed his aide to check out the nanny by questioning the staff who had hired her. The initial facts he received later that same morning were disturbing enough to fix his ebony brows into a brooding frown. He studied the small photo of Elinor Tempest: she had long hair that was a particularly vibrant shade of red, a creamy English rose complexion and exotic green eyes. Certainly, even though Jasim had never found that strange colour of hair attractive, his brother's nanny was at the very least unusual and strikingly pretty.

Worryingly, however, Elinor Tempest had not won an interview for her job by appearing on the select list of trusted nannies advanced by the employment agency engaged for the purpose. Indeed, it was unlikely that the girl would ever have made it on her own merits as she was only twenty years old and had had little work experience. Evidently, Murad had personally put forward the girl's name and insisted that she be interviewed. That startling fact put his brother's relationship with the young woman onto an altogether more questionable level. Jasim was taken aback and angered by what he was finding out. How could Murad set up such a situation beneath his own roof? And what sort of young woman accepted a position from a libidinous married man and encouraged his advances? Was Yaminah wrong? Was Murad already sexually involved with his daughter's nanny?

Repugnance engulfed Jasim. His strong principles revolted against such a sordid association in the vicinity of his innocent sister-in-law and niece. He had already learnt to his own cost that the royal status and oil wealth of the Rais family made both him and his brother targets for the most unscrupulous gold-diggers, eager to use their guile and their seductive bodies to enrich themselves. Murad had already suffered several blackmail attempts that had required police intervention. Yet, once again, his brother was recklessly running the risk of an explosive scandal, whose aftershocks would reverberate all the way home to Quaram and rock the very foundation of the monarchy.

There and then, Jasim reached a cool and snappy decision. When a crisis arose he liked to deal with it quickly. His firmly modelled lips compressed, he lifted his dark imperious head high. He would spend the weekend at Woodrow Court and size up the situation. One way or another, he would rid Yaminah's household of this calculating little slut who was threatening everything that he held dear…

'My word, what came over you?' As Louise took in Elinor's fashionable appearance her pale blue eyes rounded with surprise below her brown fringe. 'You usually dress like somebody's granny!'

Elinor winced at that blunt condemnation, her bright green eyes veiling. She supposed her lifelong reluctance to be bold in the fashion stakes dated back to her father's poisonous attacks on any garment that outlined her curves or showed her knees. A university professor and an unrepentant intellectual snob, Ernest Tempest had always been a ferociously critical parent to his only child. Only now that she was living away from home was Elinor able to spread her wings and relax, but she was the first to admit that, but for the encouragement of a shrewd and attentive saleswoman, she would not even have dared to try on the garment, never mind buy it.

Elinor strove to recall the mirror reflection that had reassured her earlier that evening. The dress's neat fit had seemed to emphasise her willowy curves but it did display a generous length of her shapely legs. Beneath her companion's critical gaze, Elinor raised an uncertain hand to its glittering beaded neckline. 'I just fell in love with it.'

Louise rolled her eyes and said drily, 'Well, you can certainly afford to lash out in the fashion stakes these days. How *is* life in the royal family of Quaram? You must be stacking up the cash in an offshore account by now.'

'You must be joking,' Elinor hastened to declare. 'And it isn't money for jam. I *do* work extremely long hours—'

'Nonsense! You've only the one kid to look after and she's at nursery school,' Louise protested as she thrust a tumbler full of liquid into Elinor's hand. 'Drink up! You're not allowed to be a party-pooper at your own twenty-first birthday bash!'

Elinor sipped at the sickly sweet concoction even though it wasn't to her taste. She didn't want to get off on the wrong foot with hot-tempered Louise, who was quick to see any form of alcoholic sobriety as a personal challenge. Both women had trained as nannies at the same college and remained friends afterwards, but Elinor was uneasily aware of the undertones in the atmosphere. It had taken months for Louise to find a decent job and she had very much resented Elinor's good fortune in the same field.

'How is work?' Louise prompted.

'The prince and his wife often go abroad or spend weekends in London and I'm left in full charge of Zahrah at Woodrow, so time off—or the lack of it—is a problem. In fact sometimes I feel more like her mother than her nanny,' Elinor confided ruefully. 'I attend everything on her behalf…even the events at her school.'

'There's got to be some drawback to all that lovely cash you're earning!' Louise commented tartly.

'Nothing's ever perfect.' Elinor shrugged with the easy tolerance of someone accustomed to an imperfect world. 'The rest of the staff are from Quaram and speak their own language, so it's quite a lonely household to live in as well. Shall we get going? Our transport awaits us.'

When Prince Murad had realised it was her birthday, he had presented Elinor with free vouchers for an upmarket London nightclub and had insisted that she make use of a chauffeur-driven limousine to travel into London. The same vehicle would also waft her home at the end of the evening.

'A twenty-first birthday only comes once in a lifetime,' Zahrah's father had pointed out cheerfully. 'Make the most of being young. Time moves cruelly fast. On my twenty-first, my father took me hawking in the desert and instructed me on what I should never forget when I became King in his place.' A wry expression had crossed the older man's visage. 'It did not occur to me then that thirty years on I would still be waiting in the wings. Not that I would have it any other way, of course; my honoured father is a very wise ruler and any man would struggle to follow his example.'

Prince Murad was a benevolent man, Elinor acknowledged reflectively. She admired the older man's strong sense of the family values of love, trust and loyalty. After her mother's death when she was ten years old, Elinor's upbringing had conspicuously lacked such sterling qualities and she was still feeling the pain of that loss. If only her own father had had an ounce of the prince's warm and kindly nature!

While Louise squealed with delight at first sight of the luxurious limousine, Elinor was thinking instead about her father's lifelong lack of interest in her. No matter how hard she had studied, her exam grades had never been good enough to please him. He had often told her that he was ashamed of her stupidity and that she was a severe disappointment to him. Her decision to become a nanny had outraged him and he had called her 'A glorified nursemaid, nothing better than a servant!' The dark shadows of those unhappy years had for ever marked her and she often felt as if she had no family at all. After all, her father had remarried without inviting her to his wedding and seemed to prefer to act as if he were childless.

'I was reading an article about Prince Murad in a magazine,' Louise remarked. 'There were hints that he has quite an eye for the ladies and that he's had affairs on the side. Watch your step with the old boy!'

Elinor frowned. 'Oh, he's definitely *not* like that with me—he's more sort of fatherly—'

'Don't be so naïve. Ninety-nine per cent of middle-aged men are lechers with young attractive women,' Louise derided with a scornful smile. 'And if you remind him of your mother…'

'I don't think that's very likely,' Elinor interrupted in some amusement. 'Mum was small, blonde and blue-eyed and I don't look one bit like her.'

'Whatever.' Louise shrugged. 'But if you didn't remind him of your mother, why the heck did he offer you—a total stranger—the job of taking care of his precious daughter?'

'It wasn't quite as easy as you make it sound,' Elinor fielded uncomfortably. 'The prince put my name forward, but I went through the same recruitment process as everybody else that applied. He said he wanted to help me out because my mother once meant something to him. He also thought I'd be young enough to appeal to his daughter as a companion. And don't forget that his wife only speaks Arabic and French, so my fluent French comes in very useful. I agree that getting the job was an extraordinary piece of good luck for me but there was nothing more sinister to it.'

Louise was still staring stonily at the younger woman. 'But *would* you sleep with him—if he asked you?'

'No, of course I wouldn't! For goodness' sake, he's almost as old as my dad!' Elinor objected with a shiver of distaste.

'Now if it was his brother, Prince Jasim, you wouldn't be shivering,' Louise quipped. 'There was a picture of him in the same article. He's sex on legs: over six foot tall, single and movie-star handsome.'

'Is he? I haven't met him.' Elinor turned her head away to look out of the limo at the well-lit city streets. Louise's persistence and murky insinuations had annoyed her. Why were people always so willing to think the worst? Elinor would not have dreamt of working for Prince Murad and his wife if there had been anything questionable in the older man's attitude towards her. Anyway, an unfortunate incident during her months of previous work experience had made Elinor very wary of flirtatious male employers.

'A shame that the brother who's going to be King one day should be short, balding and portly,' Louise commented snidely. 'Although plenty of women wouldn't let that get in the way of their ambition.'

'The fact that he's married would be enough to deter me,' Elinor replied very drily.

'It's got to be a shaky marriage though, with only a little girl to show for all those years he's been with his wife,' Louise insisted. 'I'm surprised he hasn't divorced her when there's no male heir for the next generation—'

'But there *is* an heir—the prince's younger brother,' Elinor pointed out.

'He has to be the real catch in the family, then.' A calculating glint shone in Louise's gaze. 'But after three months you still haven't met him, even though you're living in *his* house with his relatives, so that's not too promising.'

Elinor didn't waste her breath pointing out that falling in love with an Arab prince hadn't done her late mother, Rose, any favours. Rose had met Murad at university and they had fallen head over heels in love. Elinor still had the engagement ring that Murad had given her mother. The young couple's happiness had proved short-lived, however, because Murad had been threatened with disinheritance and exile if he married a foreigner. He had eventually returned to Quaram to act the dutiful son and do as he was told, while Rose had ended up marrying Ernest Tempest on the rebound. The marriage of two such ill-matched people had proved deeply unhappy.

'You haven't got any foreign travel out of the job either,' Louise reminded her sourly. 'At least I got ten days out in Cyprus with my family.'

'I'm not that fussed about travelling,' Elinor heard herself lie, her irritation at her companion's snide remarks and put-downs strong enough to make her wonder why she had bothered to maintain such a one-sided friendship.

In the exclusive club they were treated to free drinks on the strength of Prince Murad's vouchers, which was just as well as they could never have afforded to pay the high bar prices. Elinor reminded herself that it *was* her birthday and tried to shake off the sense of disappointment that had dogged her all week.

Her job was a lonely one and she often craved adult company; she knew that she needed to make the most out of a rare night out. Although she had the use of a car, Woodrow Court was deep in the Kentish countryside and within easy reach of few attractions beyond a small town. Zahrah's parents travelled a great deal and preferred to leave their daughter at home rather than disrupt her schooling. As a result, Elinor had found her own freedom severely curtailed, as when her employers were absent they expected their nanny to be in constant attendance on their child. Elinor was travelling back to Woodrow Court in a limo later because leaving her charge in the care of the household staff overnight was not an option the prince was willing to allow. Even so, after being exposed to Louise's bitter comments, Elinor was no longer feeling deprived by the fact that she had been denied the chance of a girlie sleepover.

'You're already getting the eye,' Louise sighed enviously.

Elinor tensed and refused to look in the same direction. She found socialising with the opposite sex a challenging and often humiliating experience. She was unusually tall and made six feet even in modest heels. Guys happy to chat her up while she was sitting down wanted to run once she unfurled her giraffe-long legs and stood up to tower over them. Men, she had learnt from her awkward adolescent years when she was frequently a wallflower, preferred small dainty women at whom they could look down and feel tall beside. She knew she had an attractive face and a good figure, but neither counted for anything against her ungainly height. While men noticed her, they rarely approached her.

Some hours later she said goodbye to Louise, who had picked up an admirer. Elinor, on the other hand, had experienced a particularly painful evening when a young man had come up to her table to ask her to join him and then snarled, 'Forget it!' the instant she'd got up and he'd realised in horror that he barely reached her shoulder. He and his mates had heckled her and sniggered for what remained of the night as if she were a freak at a sideshow. As a result, she had had a little too much to drink to power the nonchalant expression she'd been forced to put on to conceal her misery.

She heaved a deep-felt sigh of relief when the limo turned down the long, winding, tree-lined drive to Woodrow Court. It passed between the towers of the imposing arched gatehouse entrance into a gravelled courtyard that stretched the length of the magnificent Tudor house. It struck her that there were more lights burning than usual. She climbed out and the cool evening air went to her head as much as the alcohol had earlier. She sucked in a sustaining breath in an effort to clear her swimming head and struggled to nego-tiate a straight path to the front door that was already opening for her.

Her steps weaved around a little as she crossed the echoing hall. A man was emerging from the library and her attention locked straight on to him. He was a stranger and so absolutely beautiful that one glance deprived her of oxygen and brain power. She came to a wobbly halt to stare. Black hair was swept back from his brow, bronzed skin stretched taut over his high slashing cheekbones, arrogant nose and aggressive jaw line. There was some-thing uniquely compelling about his lean, arrestingly handsome features. He had gorgeous eyes, dark, deep set and bold, and when he stepped below the overhead chande-lier they burned a pure hot gold. Her heart started to hammer as if she were sprinting.

Jasim was not in a good mood. He had not been amused when he'd arrived for the weekend only to discover that his brother and sister-in-law and even his quarry were all out and unavailable, making his presence as an interested onlooker somewhat superfluous. 'Miss Tempest?'

'Er…yes?' Elinor reached out a trembling hand to brace herself on the carved pedestal at the foot of the massive wooden staircase. He had a gorgeous face that inexplicably continued to draw her attention like a powerful magnet. She just wanted to stare and stare. 'Sorry, you…are?'

'Prince Murad's brother, Jasim,' he breathed, surveying her with forbidding cool, in spite of the powerfully masculine interest she fired in him.

He immediately wanted to know if she looked at his brother in the same awestruck way. Any man might be flattered by a woman looking at him with a wonder more worthy of a supernatural being. In the flesh, Elinor Tempest was, he already appreciated, a much more dangerous entity than he had ever imagined she might be. In a dress that hugged the sensual swell of her breasts and revealed her incredibly long legs, she was out-and-out stunning. Hair that had looked garishly bright in the photo was, in reality, a rich dark auburn and a crowning glory that hung in a luxuriant curling tangle halfway down her back. Only the finest emeralds could have equalled the amazing green of her eyes. With that spectacular hair, those wide eyes and a lush pink mouth set against flawless creamy skin, she was literally the stuff of male fantasy. It was a challenging instant before Jasim, universally renowned for his cool head, could concentrate his thoughts again.

'You appear to be drunk,' Jasim breathed icily, his stern intonation roughened by the disturbing hardening at his groin as his body reacted involuntarily to the sexually appealing vision she made.

Colour flared in Elinor's cheeks. 'P-possibly…er…a little bit,' she stammered in great discomfiture, dragging in a long deep breath that made the rounded mounds of her breasts shimmy beneath the fine fabric of her dress. 'I don't usually drink much but it was a special occasion.'

Jasim was finding it a challenge to keep his attention above her chin. 'If you worked for me, I would not tolerate you appearing in this state.'

'Luckily I'm not working for you,' Elinor flipped back, before she could think better of it. 'Nor am I working at this precise moment. I'm on my own time. I had the evening off—'

'Nevertheless, while you live beneath this roof I consider such conduct unacceptable.'

Elinor registered that he had drawn closer and that she actually had to tip back her head to take all of him in. He was very tall, she noted belatedly, at least six feet four inches, considerably taller than his older brother. In fact there was nothing about him that reminded her of Prince Murad, for Jasim was broad-shouldered and muscular in build. He carried not an ounce of excess weight on his lean, lithe physique. Of course, the two men were only half-brothers, she recalled, born to different mothers.

'What if Zahrah was to wake up and see you in such a condition?' Jasim demanded, meeting her intense gaze with his own and stiffening at the rampant response of his body to her encouragement. If that was how she looked at his brother, he totally understood how Murad could have been tempted off the straight and narrow. The ripe fullness of her soft pink mouth was a sensual invitation all on its own.

'The nurse who has been with Zahrah since she was

born sleeps next door to her. I think you're being very unreasonable,' Elinor told him tightly.

Jasim was staggered by that disrespectful rejoinder and decided that she was utterly without shame. Nor had it escaped his notice that she apparently had a limousine at her private disposal. That was a flagrant display of his brother's special favour, which could only add weight to Yaminah's worst fears. 'Is this how you speak to my brother?'

'Your brother, who *is* my employer, is a great deal more pleasant and less critical. I don't work for you and I'm entitled to a social life,' Elinor declared, her chin at a defiant tilt even though she could feel a tension headache building like a painful band of steel round her temples. Her self-esteem, already battered by the treatment she had earlier withstood at the nightclub, refused to bear any more in saintly silence. 'And now, if you don't mind, I'd like to go to bed.'

Jasim only knew in that moment of red-hot outrage at her impertinence that he wanted to take her to that bed, spread her across it and make love to her until she begged him for more and ached from his passion. As he struggled to master the fierce desire threatening his usually rigid self-control he was shocked by the sheer novelty of a lust that powerful. No woman ever came between Jasim and his wits, not even the one he had once briefly planned to marry. But as he watched Elinor Tempest endeavour to mount the stairs without swaying and stumbling from the effects of the alcohol she had consumed, he knew that he would know no peace until he had bedded her and made her his.

Her foot, shod in a sandal with a thin slippery sole, slid off a step and she lurched back with a cry of alarm breaking from her lips as she clutched frantically at the solid balustrade for support.

'Safety is yet another reason why you shouldn't drink like this,' Jasim breathed hatefully close, a splayed hand like an iron bar bracing her spine to prevent her from falling backwards down the stairs.

'I don't need your help,' Elinor protested furiously, sliding off her shoes to ensure there were no further accidents and gathering them together in one impatient hand. 'I hate people who preach.... I bet you say, "I told you so", as well!'

The scent of her hair and her skin assailed Jasim in an evocative wave of sensuous appeal. She smelt like peaches and made him think of hot sunlight and even hotter sex. He was convinced that she would be a willing partner. Her style of dress and her behaviour had already persuaded him that she was far from being an innocent. Murad was much too trusting to be left at the mercy of his own lust and the manipulations of a rapacious youthful temptress. Elinor Tempest, Jasim decided, was a justifiable target for his calculating plan to bring about her downfall. Striving to keep the lid on his temper and his libido, he urged her upstairs.

'All right…I'll be fine now,' Elinor muttered as she reached her comfortable bedroom. The defiance was steadily seeping out of her, for she was exhausted and her spirits were low. 'You've been the perfect conclusion to a truly horrible birthday and now, *please*, I'd like to be left alone.'

Jasim subjected her to a measured assessment from the doorway. Alienating her was not a good idea. What had he been thinking of? Desire was pulsing through him and already as much entrenched there as the beat of the blood through his veins. He wanted her and once he took her to his bed Murad would turn his back on her. Taking her to bed would not be a sacrifice. Picturing her there with those flame-coloured curls loose and her eyes soft with longing offered him the prospect of a sweeter and more sensual pleasure than he had ever dreamt he might find in so pre-meditated an encounter.

Conservation needs had put the thrill of the hunt out of reach in Quaram and Jasim had long missed the excitement. He discovered that he could hardly wait for the satisfying conclusion of what promised to be a most enjoyable sexual game. It did not once occur to him that he might fail to get her into his bed—since he had never yet met with a refusal…

CHAPTER TWO

THE next morning, while Elinor showered, she turned clammy with horror when she recalled her dialogue with Prince Jasim. Alcohol had made an idiot of her! She should have been more careful about how much she'd drunk. But then it was six months since she had even tasted alcohol, she thought, biting anxiously at her lower lip. Furthermore she had been resentful about the fact that she couldn't just have a couple of days off when she asked for them and a taste of youthful freedom.

But not so resentful that she wanted to lose her very well-paid job, she reflected worriedly, a job, moreover, which would add solid-gold appeal to her CV when she went off in pursuit of her next position. No, the very last thing she needed now was to get sacked for being cheeky to a prince! She hadn't even called him 'sir' when she'd addressed him and she bit back a moan at the recollection. She was usually so sensible and polite. Why hadn't she kept her tongue between her teeth? The truth was that she had been in a bad mood and the unhappy combination of his undeniable good looks and fanciability, followed by his cutting criticism, had proved the proverbial last straw. She already knew from hearing Prince Murad erupt when the smallest thing annoyed him that royal egos were eggshell thin and super-sensitive and royal tempers quick to ignite. Prince Jasim would never forgive her for being rude to him and he was certain to complain to his brother.

It was a Saturday and Zahrah had a riding lesson. While her charge was being taught, Elinor usually went riding as well since she was an accomplished horsewoman and the stables contained an enviable selection of mounts. She pulled on her shabby navy breeches, a lemon T-shirt and finally her boots. She was about to leave her bedroom when a knock sounded on the door. She opened it and was startled when a big basket of beautifully arranged flowers was presented to her by one of the manservants.

At first Elinor couldn't believe the magnificent flowers were for her and she drank in the heady scent of the glorious pink roses with a blissful sigh before she detached the card envelope and opened it.

'Happy belated birthday wishes and my apologies, Jasim'

Elinor was stunned. *He* was apologising to *her*? He was even wishing her a happy birthday and giving her flowers? Her jaw was ready to crash to the floor in disbelief. She summoned up a misty image of him. As well as being more beautiful than any man had the right to be, Prince Jasim had impressed her as being arrogant, autocratic and very proud. He definitely hadn't struck her as being the apologising type. In fact she had seen him more as the sort of guy who always had the last word and a disparaging one at that.

But obviously first impressions had been kind to neither of them the night before. It was the first time a man had given Elinor flowers and she was hopelessly impressed and pleased by the gesture because she really had had a lousy, disappointing birthday. Zahrah raced into the room. Bubbling with life, the four-year-old was a pretty child with a mop of silky dark curls and sparkling brown eyes.

'Morning, Elinor!' Zahrah carolled, giving her an affectionate hug. 'Are you coming for breakfast now?'

They went downstairs and Elinor was about to head for the small dining room where she usually ate with the child when Ahmed, the major domo of the household, intercepted her. Zahrah acted as translator and informed Elinor that they were having breakfast with her Uncle Jasim today. They were ushered into the massive formal dining room.

Zahrah let out a yelp of excitement and bowled down the room to throw herself into Jasim's arms. It gave Elinor a minute to compose herself as Jasim, having thrown down his newspaper, rose from the table to greet their arrival. In the full light flooding through the tall windows, his bronzed aristocratic face was startlingly handsome and once again she discovered that she found it virtually impossible to look away from him. He dominated the room with his powerful presence and she was hooked afresh by a fevered compulsion to study those lean classic features, still driven to try and work out what it was about them that repeatedly drew her attention. Her heart was already pounding, making it hard for her to breathe levelly. Then he smiled down at the child in his arms and the high-voltage force of his charismatic attraction hit her like a rod of lightning striking the ground.

'Miss Tempest…' he murmured lazily as he swung out a chair beside his own. Clad in tailored riding gear, he looked outrageously elegant and sophisticated. 'Please join us.'

Elinor had to force herself to walk down the length of the table to join him in a seat a good deal closer than she would have chosen for herself. She was flustered. Butterflies were fluttering in her tummy and she didn't know what to do with her hands any more. She felt ridiculously like a schoolgirl, self-conscious and silly and awkward, all at the same time. 'Thank you for the flowers. You were very generous,' she muttered in a rush, keen to get the acknowledgement out of the way while Zahrah was busy chattering to Ahmed about her favourite cereal.

The brilliant ebony eyes screened by dense black lashes rested on her and she honestly thought her heart might stop beating altogether. 'It was nothing.'

'I owe you an apology...I was rude,' she framed.

'A novel experience for me,' the prince purred like a sleek panther being stroked.

For a split second Elinor wanted to slap him rather than stroke him for not giving a more gracious response to her attempt to make amends. 'Nobody ever answers you back? Or quarrels with you?' she heard herself query.

'Nobody,' Jasim confirmed as if that was a perfectly normal state of affairs. He watched her glance up at him from below her feathery lashes, a delicate flush of colour on her cheeks, and thought what a class act she was putting on for his benefit. He could hardly credit that it was the same woman, for no hint of the strident, argumentative redhead he had met the night before was on show. Everything about her this morning from her show of apparent unease to her soft tone of voice and her girlish reluctance to meet his eyes shouted the kind of shy uncertainty and sexual innocence that was most likely to ensnare an older man. No wonder his brother was upsetting his wife over the scheming little slut, he reflected grimly. The act didn't work quite so well on Jasim. But then he was rather more sophisticated than Murad and better attuned to the liberal sexual mores of Elinor Tempest's age group. As Yaminah had doubtless intended when she invited Jasim for a weekend while she and his brother were elsewhere, Jasim intended to make full and immediate use of the clear field she had given him.

'More coffee?' Jasim snapped long brown fingers with a natural assumption of command that seemed to come as instinctively as breathing to him. On immediate alert, a servant surged forward with alacrity to refresh the coffee cups. Zahrah had been inclined to treat Elinor the same way, until Elinor had taught the little girl otherwise. Even so, Elinor had daily exposure to the reality that members of the Quarami royal family were one step down from Divinity in the eyes of those who waited on them.

'Tell me why your birthday was horrible,' Jasim instructed silkily, studying her with those stunning dark eyes and relaxing back into his chair with the confident air of a male awaiting the commencement of the entertainment.

A pulse beating somewhere at the base of her throat and her nerves reacting like jumping beans, Elinor had grown very tense. 'That wouldn't be appropriate, sir.'

The dense black lashes lifted over frowning deep golden eyes. 'I decide what is appropriate,' he told her in immediate contradiction. *'Talk.'*

For an instant Elinor was astonished by that imperious command delivered with the absolute expectation of a male accustomed to instant obedience. It was a relief when Zahrah stole the moment with her nonsensical chatter.

'You can explain later.' Jasim delivered the reprieve over his niece's downbent head. 'I'm coming down to the stables with you and Zahrah.'

The prospect unnerved Elinor and she looked up at him again and froze at the hungry light in his measuring gaze before hurriedly glancing down at her coffee again. Shock decimated her appetite for her toast, while her tummy performed an enervating series of little somersaults. His close scrutiny might suggest that he found her attractive, but she could not believe that a prince could have developed a personal interest in her and scolded herself for letting her imagination take flight. Perhaps he was more like his kindly brother than she had appreciated and was simply keen to smooth over the unpleasantness of their first encounter.

Ahmed secured Zahrah in a child's seat in the back of a glossy black Range Rover. Elinor climbed into the passenger seat and watched Jasim stroll round the bonnet. Even with his black hair tousled by the breeze he was as strikingly sleek and beautiful as a bronzed angel. She met his eyes through the windscreen and suddenly she was wildly, hopelessly aware of her own body. Her full breasts felt constrained inside her bra and an odd little clenching sensation low in her pelvis made her shift uneasily in her seat. She was shocked, for she hadn't realised that being drawn to a man could be such a physical experience, that her body could feel as if it were all revved up for a race. Mortified colour mantled her cheeks. A lean brown long-fingered hand as wondrously well-proportioned as the rest of him depressed the handbrake and the engine fired.

'Are you fond of horses?' Jasim enquired.

'I've been mad about them since I was a kid,' Elinor confessed with a rueful laugh. 'I started riding lessons at the same age as Zahrah. A neighbour kept stables and I used to go there and help out after school.'

'Have you ever had a horse of your own?'

Elinor tensed and her face fell. 'Yes, from the age of nine to fourteen. My father sold her then. He thought the time I spent with Starlight was interfering with my studies—'

'You must've been upset.'

'I was devastated.' Elinor folded her lips, unable to find adequate words to explain just how shattering a blow that sudden loss had been to her. Her father had not even warned her of his intentions and she had not got the chance to say goodbye to the horse she'd loved. Starlight had also been her last link with her late mother and her only real friend, the one element in her wretchedly unhappy teen years that had kept her going through thick and thin. 'But she was still a young horse and I'm sure she went to some other girl to be absolutely adored all over again.'

'It sounds as though your father was very strict,' Jasim remarked, keen to extract more information from her. He was not at all surprised that the very first thing she should tell him should be a sob story guaranteed to paint her in a sympathetic light.

'*Too* strict. After that, I wasn't allowed any interests at all outside school. It was a relief to leave home,' Elinor admitted ruefully, thinking of the release of no longer having to live daily with constant wounding criticism and reproaches for her unacceptable exam results. Although greater maturity had enabled her to appreciate that she had simply been an average student rather than a completely stupid one, her father had made her feel like a hopeless failure at the tender age of sixteen years and her self-esteem had still to recover from his abrasive style of parenting.

Jasim's sculpted sensual mouth tightened as once again she confirmed his suspicions about her true nature. He recalled the widening invitation of her expressive and artful eyes as she met his gaze, the revealingly taut points of her nipples that were currently showing through her T-shirt. She was certainly very responsive and he found her inability to conceal her reaction to him very, very sexy.

A decent parent, however, would naturally have sought to impose restrictions on so free-spirited a daughter, he reasoned, expecting to feel disgusted at the mounting proof of her probable promiscuity. Instead he tensed at the heavy arousal stirring at his groin and cursed the ready sexual heat that afflicted him in Elinor Tempest's company. Only sexual satisfaction would take care of that problem and he had no intention of practising patience, nor even the suspicion that patience would prove necessary. Mindful of his niece's presence, he concentrated on *not* thinking about how thoroughly Elinor would be persuaded to ease the demands of his high-voltage sex drive.

'I'll give you a tour of the stud farm,' Jasim drawled.

As they were early for Zahrah's lesson, Elinor made no protest and indeed her interest quickened at the prospect of a special viewing in the owner's company, because although she often visited the stables to ride she had stayed away from the stud. It was a large impressive operation housed in immaculately maintained buildings, complete with all-weather gallops and paddocks, and it was heavily staffed. The manager hurried out of the office to greet Jasim. The resident vet and other senior staff soon joined them. Keen though she was on horses, the dialogue soon ranged beyond Elinor's knowledge with talk of racing prospects and recent wins on the turf. Some way through it, she left to check that Zahrah's horse was saddled up. The little girl's instructor arrived soon afterwards.

'Will you be taking Amaranth out?' the groom asked Elinor then.

'Yes, please.' A huge smile on her face, Elinor went to greet the big brown gelding impatiently shifting in his box as he recognised the sound of her voice. She petted him and led him out. It had taken a month of regular visits for the head groom to trust her with the more lively mounts. The freedom to ride pretty much whenever she liked and without cost was yet another good reason why she wanted to hang on to her job.

In the midst of trying to disengage from his staff, Jasim saw her ride out and his ebony brows shot up. 'You let the nanny ride Amaranth?' he demanded in a tone of censure.

'Elinor is well able to control him, Your Highness,' the head groom responded. 'She's a terrific rider.'

At that moment Jasim received the perfect opportunity to see that truth for himself as she spurred the spirited gelding towards a fence, soaring over it with a grace and ease that impressed even him.

Elinor heard the thump of pursuing hooves and turned her head. On the back of his powerful black stallion, Mercury, Jasim was catching up on her fast. Her chin came up and she urged Amaranth on in a flat-out race across the lush rolling acres of parkland that made Woodrow Court such a paradise for a horse lover.

Jasim was stunned that she had the nerve to challenge him, for he had expected her to come to a halt and wait for him. He rarely rode in female company because women tended to cling to him like superglue and chatter and flirt continually, behaviour that interfered with his relaxation. In comparison, Elinor gave him the opportunity to chase her and he appreciated that her control of her mount and her skill were worthy of his respect.

Amaranth ran out of steam by the lake and Elinor reined him in and dismounted below some trees. Jasim was talking on a cell phone as he rode up on Mercury. He slid down to the ground with effortless grace and watched her remove her riding cap, releasing the piled up mass of her hair in a silken tangle of luxuriance and stretching in a movement that delineated every curve and ensured that her generous little breasts strained beneath her T-shirt. Although he was convinced it was a deliberate move to attract his attention to her body, that cheap little trick still worked on him. Indeed desire knifed through him, making him hot and hard within seconds. Conscious of the reality that the breeches would conceal nothing, he peeled off his cap and strode over to the edge of the lake, willing the tumult of his rampant hormones back under control. He was furious and knocked off balance by a loss of self-discipline that he had not experienced since the years of adolescence.

Elinor looked across the lake and rejoiced in the early summer lushness and the natural beauty of her surroundings. Although she sometimes felt isolated at Woodrow, she had no desire to exchange the countryside and the sense of well-being it gave her for the noise and buzz of the city.

'You're an excellent rider,' Jasim murmured levelly.

Helpless amusement sparkled in her green eyes as she sensed that she had irritated him. 'You'd have beaten me hollow on Mercury if I hadn't had such a head start.'

His keen attention was welded to her. He wasn't used to being teased and he was so bone-deep competitive that he was accustomed to coming first in every field of his busy life. Even his best friend could not have called him a good loser. Yet confronted by the captivating mixture of mischief and artless innocence that momentarily shone in her smile, his exasperation vanished. He was seeing, he told himself harshly, what his brother had to see in her. Even though it was undoubtedly a fake front put on to attract, it was also indisputably effective when a guy as cynical as he was about women started questioning his view of her.

Her skin warming below the intensity of his stare, Elinor drank in the fresh air and decided that being alone with Jasim in such circumstances was likely to cause the kind of talk that would only damage her standing in an old-fashioned household. 'I'd better get back. Zahrah's lesson will be over soon.'

'Her nurse is coming down from the house to collect her. I've ordered refreshments for us…ah, there they are now.'

Her lower lip had fallen away from the upper as she turned to follow his gaze and saw an estate Land Rover trundling towards them across the grass. 'You ordered refreshments for us…to be served out here?'

His satiric sable brows pleated. 'Why not?'

His disregard of the obvious was superb and he managed to magnify her awareness of the huge inequality between them. She was also taken aback that he should re-organise her day by calling in her charge's nurse to take care of her when she herself could perfectly have done so. After all, looking after Zahrah was her job. But her surprise had been replaced by pure amazement at his casual announcement that refreshments were to be served in the middle of the park at his request. He saw nothing strange in the indulgence, she realised, for, like his royal brother, expecting immediate fulfilment of his every command was as normal to Jasim as disappointment and compromise were to her.

Staff emerged from the vehicle at the double and an array of hot and cold drinks, china, glasses and snacks were laid out while an exquisite wool rug was spread across the grass. Elinor, who had dimly expected a picnic-style metal mug to be thrust into her hand, was nonplussed once again. Jasim drank only water. She watched his sensationally attractive face hollow as he drank and swallowed, noticed how the sunlight glimmered across his hard bronzed cheekbones and reflected off black hair that the breeze had ruffled into faint curls. Her throat felt tight. Seated on the rug while he lounged back against the tree with the pure animal fluidity that distinguished his every move, she sipped awkwardly at her coffee in its elegant china cup.

'Now you can tell me why your birthday was a disappointment,' Jasim decreed.

'I hoped you would forget about that comment,' Elinor confided.

Jasim flashed her a mocking smile that tilted her heart on its axis and made her feel so warm that she was momentarily afraid that she might spontaneously combust. Unable to take her eyes off him, she explained about the nightclub tickets, while wondering why his handsome bone structure seemed to tighten when she praised his brother's kindness.

'Murad is a very generous employer.' Her admission was yet another nail in her coffin as far as Jasim was concerned, as he saw in it good reason for Yaminah's concern. He could not credit that such favouritism could be innocent, or that its recipient had not deliberately flirted and coaxed her way into his brother's notice and regard. He even understood why Murad had put a family limo at her disposal. His brother had naturally wished to ensure that she came back to Woodrow at the end of the evening.

'Yes, but I'm not that fussed about nightclubs,' Elinor admitted. 'I never meet anyone anyway, I'm far too tall for most men—'

'But exactly the right height for me,' Jasim inserted softly, his dark accented drawl roughening the vowel sounds in a way that sent a responsive quiver down her taut spinal cord.

Perturbed by that personal comment, Elinor reddened. 'Well, I find being this tall an embarrassment.'

Jasim stretched down a hand. 'Stand up. Let me see you.'

Setting down her cup with a noisy rattle that betrayed her confusion, Elinor clasped his hand and he levered her upright. For a long timeless moment eyes as dark as liquid oil, richly enhanced by inky, spiky lashes of inordinate length, inspected her hectically flushed face. She leant her hips back against the tree trunk for support because her knees felt wobbly.

'You have fabulous long legs,' Jasim murmured, lean fingers brushing curling strands of rich red hair back from her brow. 'Glorious hair and a mouth that is a temptation to any red-blooded man.' His attention dropped in emphasis to the generous swell of her lips and so caught up was she in the power of the moment that she trembled. 'From the first instant I saw you I wanted to kiss you—'

'You were furious with me,' she contradicted, even though she was locked to the allure of his gorgeous eyes.

'It didn't stop me wondering what you would taste like.' Jasim was so close that she could barely breathe until he finally lowered his proud dark head to satisfy his curiosity.

It was a good few months since Elinor had been kissed. But never, ever had she been kissed as Jasim bin Hamid al Rais kissed her. His sheer passion blew her away. His tongue delved and dipped between her readily parted lips with sensual skill and explicit eroticism. A slow, almost painfully sweet ache awakened between her slender thighs and a slight gasp escaped her. Her nipples pinched into taut tingling buds that pushed painfully against the scratchy lace cups of her bra. Her hands clutched his shoulders to keep her upright. He rocked against her and she felt the raw urgency of his arousal and exulted in his response to her with an earthiness that startled her. All of a sudden she was finding out what it was to really want a man, and the strength of that longing shook her back into an awareness of what she was doing.

Almost the instant she reclaimed her sanity, she pulled away from him, turning to hide her face, shaking hands flying up to rake her hair out of her eyes and brush her swollen tingling mouth as if she still could not credit what she had felt. 'Sorry, this isn't right,' she muttered unevenly.

Jasim went from surprise at the apparent rejection to bleak amusement at what he saw as a clever ploy by an experienced woman. There was nothing more tantalising to a man than a brief taste of forbidden fruit followed by a maidenly show of reluctance. He too preferred the thrill of the chase to an easy surrender, but the urgency of his arousal had almost persuaded him to forget the game of sexual entrapment he was engaged in playing.

'How is it wrong?'

'I work for your family…we're worlds apart. How many reasons do you need?' she retorted in a surge of grudging candour, for the last thing she wanted to do just then was make it easier for him to walk away from her.

Jasim decided to give her what he knew she must want—the encouragement to ditch her designs on his brother and concentrate on him instead. He went in for the kill with words that were the virtual antithesis of his usual cool, un-committed approach to her sex. 'I find you incredibly attractive and I am not a snob. My great-great-grandfather was a poor but proud man when he took the throne of Quaram. I have known many women but I have never felt like this before. We *must* explore what is between us.'

Her troubled green eyes switched back to him and clung to his lean dark features. She craved that visual contact and wanted to trust in what he had said, but at the same time she was terrified of getting hurt as her mother had been in a fairy-tale romance that had swiftly crumbled and led to a lifetime of unhappy comparisons and regret.

'I don't think your brother would approve and I value my job,' Elinor framed uncertainly.

His shrewd dark-as-charcoal eyes glinted as he received what he deemed to be her most honest answer yet. Which brother was she to place her trust in? After all, she wouldn't want to fall between the proverbial two stools and end up with neither man in tow. He reached down and closed his hands firmly over hers. 'I promise you—you will come to no harm with me.'

And that heartening vow reverberated through Elinor while Jasim made easy conversation about horses on the ride back to the stables. Nothing but trouble could come from an ordinary person trifling with royalty, she told herself fiercely, but she could still taste him on her lips and she couldn't help reliving the heady excitement of that stolen embrace. Zahrah was already with her nurse when Elinor reappeared and she saw the older woman note in surprise that Jasim was with her and stare. She wondered if her mouth was as swollen as it felt and she flushed brick red with discomfiture. He insisted that she travel back to the house with him, another mark of conspicuous favour that embarrassed her.

That afternoon, Elinor clung to her usual schedule and took Zahrah out shopping and then on to a newly released children's film showing at the local cinema. As was usual on a Saturday, they ate a light supper in the nursery. She gave Zahrah her bath and tucked the little girl into bed afterwards with a fond hug. Too enervated to settle for an evening by the television, she put on her swimsuit, donned a towelling robe and headed downstairs to the indoor swimming pool. When Zahrah's parents were in residence she didn't like to use the facility unless she had Zahrah with her, but with the couple away she felt there was no harm in doing so. The pool complex was huge and spectacular, complete with a stunning waterfall and underwater jets, and a spa to one side of it.

Emerging from the lift, Jasim was impressed when he saw that Elinor was already waiting in the water for him. This was not a girl who let moss grow over an opportunity, or who was prepared to run the risk of a man losing interest from lack of exposure to her available charms. He watched her slide from the bubbling spa into the main pool, giving him a ravishing display of her slender but curvaceous body sheathed in tight purple stretchy fabric that left little to the imagination. The ripe swell of her firm little breasts and the heart-shaped femininity of her derriere were wonderfully visible and would have awakened any man's appreciation. But Jasim resented the powerful pull she exerted over him and thought that the look of surprise and self-consciousness she then assumed at first glimpse of him was an award-winning effort. What an actress she was! How many other men had she practised her wiles on? Nobody knew better than Jasim that once a woman got a man weak with lust, she could convince him of virtually anything. Bitterness assailed him as he recalled his own past.

Elinor didn't feel right staying in the pool when Jasim was in it as well. After all, it was his house and his pool and she couldn't help worrying that the other staff would think she was throwing herself at their prince if they saw her there, daring to share the same water as royalty. She climbed out and pulled on her towelling robe.

Jasim swam over to the side and heaved himself out. Water streaming in rivulets from the taut contours of his lean bronzed body, he approached her and lifted a towel. 'Why are you leaving?'

'I just think it's wiser,' Elinor mumbled tautly, trying not to let her attention linger anywhere it shouldn't while he towelled himself dry. She was grateful that he favoured loose shorts rather than body-hugging briefs.

Dark golden eyes smouldered over her and lingered on her pouting mouth. 'For whom? You want me too. Don't deny that this feeling is mutual.'

The very boldness of that statement struck hot colour into her face. She tied the sash on the robe with clumsy hands. He spoke with such terrifying confidence, and even though it scared her, his complete assurance drew her like a bonfire on an icy day. 'But it's not enough,' she protested, still trying to get a grip on a situation that felt as though it were flying fast out of her control.

Jasim closed his hands round her narrow wrists and drew her firmly to him. 'This is only the beginning…'

And she fell into the depths of the hot, hungry kiss that followed like a novice swimmer with a suicide wish as she sank deeper and deeper out of her depth. One feverish kiss led hotly into the next. He crushed her mouth with devastating urgency and her excitement rose and rose until she was shaking and shivering against him, her body on fire with her craving for more.

'This is not the place for this, but you are irresistible,' he breathed thickly against her reddened lips. Bending, he scooped her off her feet and carried her into the lift.

She had never been in the lift before, for it travelled only to the master bedroom to facilitate the early-morning swims that the owner of the house apparently enjoyed. He set her down beside the giant divan bed and pushed the loosened robe off her slim shoulders so that it fell in a heap round her bare feet. She looked up at him with sensually stunned eyes, the swollen contours of her strawberry-pink mouth like a magnet reeling him back down to her again.

'We can't do this!' she exclaimed, pushed to the edge of panic by the intimacy of the bedroom. She thought she had been very naïve in failing to appreciate that he might expect her to go to bed with him without further ado.

He tugged her hand down to the front of his wet shorts where the fabric was moulded to the massive width and length of his erection. '*Please*…I won't be able to sleep for wanting you.'

And Elinor could have withstood almost any other response but, even as he plunged her into agonies of self-conscious embarrassment, that roughened sensual appeal thrilled her to the core of her being and touched her to the heart. When had any man ever wanted her like that? When had she *ever* contrived to rouse such a storm of desire? Far more often than she cared to recall she had been made to feel freakishly tall and unfeminine. Meeting his smouldering dark golden eyes, she rejoiced in his need for her and suppressed the voice of reason urging caution and restraint at the back of her mind. Hadn't she always been sensible and controlled? Was there any real harm in taking a risk for once? Especially when she was falling for him like a ton of bricks: she affixed to that last thought, eager to be daring and worthy of such a passion as his. This might well be the *only* time in her life when a man called her 'irresistible'…

CHAPTER THREE

BEFORE Elinor could even register what Jasim was about, he had peeled down the top of her swimsuit so that the pale plump mounds of her breasts tumbled free. A low masculine growl of hunger escaped him when he saw the luscious and prominent protrusion of her rose-pink nipples. 'You have the most wonderful body.'

He kneaded those tender tips with expert fingers and she cried out in shaken acknowledgement of the arrow of sensation darting straight down to the balloon of burgeoning heat expanding low in her pelvis. That fast she was in uncharted territory and at the mercy of the hunger he had unleashed inside her. She craved more and he was not slow to answer that craving. He brought her down on the bed and closed his mouth fiercely to a straining pink crest, taking it between his teeth and toying with the tender tip until her fingers formed into claws that raked the sheet beneath her hands. A frantic sense of swollen heat between her splayed thighs was sending up her temperature and threatening what little remained of her control. He touched her there where she was most tender of all just once while he played with her lush breasts and her spine arched off the bed in a reaction so strong it almost frightened her.

'You're too tense,' he censured, wrenching her free of her swimsuit and rolling off the bed to remove his wet shorts.

Nerves and doubts immediately attacked Elinor again. Everything was going too fast for her and she was trying to work out how she could have allowed matters to go so far without seriously questioning what she was about to do. After all, sleeping with a man for the first time was a very big deal on her terms. Elinor stared at her first daunting view of a man unclothed. He seemed endowed out of all reasonable proportion to her untried body. The shameless burn at the heart of her felt as scary as it was exciting and she wondered feverishly if she was doing the right thing or simply letting passion and the joy of attracting so superlative a male go to her head.

Jasim looked down at her with an amount of pleasure that took even him aback. She looked like a goddess, he decided in awe, the fiery abundance of her hair the perfect complement to her full creamy curves. Never before had a woman made him ache with such ravenous hunger…no, not even Sophia had had that power. But he would never be vulnerable with a woman again or allow desire to overwhelm his judgement, he told himself with fierce confidence.

'I want you now,' Jasim confessed, coming down on the bed beside her, his lean powerful body taut with sexual impatience. Overwhelming desire made it an effort for him to recall that his primary motivation in taking her was to ensure she lost the power to lure his brother into an affair.

Just looking at his lean bronzed features, which were compellingly handsome and strikingly serious, Elinor felt her mouth run dry and her heart threatened to drum its way out of her chest. 'I've never felt this way before,' she whispered unevenly and held back the craven admission that feeling as she did just then was distinctly intimidating.

Immediately discarding that ingenuous assurance as a pre-planned sop voiced to stroke his male ego, Jasim bit back an appreciative sound of amusement and ravished her soft mouth afresh. Against her will, Elinor felt herself melt again. Her insecurities ebbed while every nerve ending leapt in helpless response to the scent and touch of him. He felt like living hair-roughened bronze next to her, hot and hard and strong. She had a delirious image of what it would feel like to have him inside her and was shattered at the leap of her body and the newly wanton direction of her thoughts.

Jasim rubbed the tiny bud below her mound and listened to her cry out her pleasure. She was swollen with arousal and as slippery as wet silk. With a forefinger he probed the delicate cleft and discovered that she was deliciously small and tight within. She gasped and winced and he marvelled at her theatrical ability. Of course, just like Sophia she most likely assumed that an Arab male would only properly value her if she pretended to be a virgin. Sophia had paid a small fortune to have her hymen surgically restored and he had been absolutely fooled by her masquerade, he remembered with deep bitterness.

'What's wrong?' Elinor exclaimed, glimpsing the dark shadowed look in his brilliant eyes at the breathless peak of a rippling wave of almost torturous pleasure. His lovemaking enthralled her, but now she wondered if he had finally registered her lack of experience. Was that a turn-off for him?

'Nothing could be wrong…'

'I've never slept with anyone else,' Elinor admitted awkwardly. 'Is that a problem?'

'How could it be, when you are about to honour me beyond all other men?' The sardonic light in his gaze hardened at her careful last-minute assurance of her sexual innocence. Afraid that he might not get the message, she was leaving nothing to chance. He was wild for the hot, tight satisfaction of her body under his, but he would have preferred the cool self-restraint to tell her that she was a liar and that her shoddy, foolish pretence didn't fool him for a moment.

He settled into the cradle of her thighs and he was so eager for her that little tremors were racking his lean, muscular frame. He pushed into her moist, warm entrance and revelled in the taut feel and softness of her silky inner passage. Driven by a ferocious sense of need, he thrust back her thighs to deepen his penetration and at the same instant that he ensured she stretched to accommodate all of him she vented a sharp cry of pain. He froze, not having expected her to go to town on the virgin act to this extent.

Elinor was mortified. 'I'm sorry, it just hurt a bit…it's all right,' she muttered, her mortification so great that she wanted the bed to open up and swallow her.

'It is for me to apologise. I should have been more gentle,' Jasim breathed, marvelling that he could match her masquerade, all the while inching his aching shaft into the velvet-smooth honeyed welcome at the heart of her.

As her discomfort receded the excitement came back in steady increments that were stoked by every skilled move he made. Elinor gasped and wrapped her arms round him and discovered he could once again be the giver of such energising sensation as she had never dared to dream existed. The pace quickened to a hypnotic tempo and she was swept away by the erotic excitement of his sensual rhythm. The sweet surges of pleasure ran closer and closer together, driving her to the very peak of an explosive climax and then tipping her off the edge into a blissful weightless fall and satiated indolence.

Jasim stared down at her in the aftermath, his dark eyes blazing gold with passionate appreciation. 'You took me to paradise and I have never been there with a woman before.'

As he held her to him, his heart pounding against hers, Elinor blinked back sudden tears, for she felt very emotional. She also felt incredibly tender towards him and strung a line of kisses across a broad brown shoulder. She fiercely fought off the sense of shame and awkwardness that she guiltily knew was waiting to pounce on her. He made her feel special and she was desperate to hold on to that reassuring sensation.

'I should go back to my own room,' she mumbled, however, a few minutes later.

Jasim's arms tightened like bars of steel round her. He had every intention of fully satisfying his desire for her. 'Tonight you are mine and you stay here with me,' he spelt out thickly.

And she *was* his now, he reflected in male triumph, his hungry body already quickening against hers again. One stolen night, however, was all he could dare to take beneath a roof that also housed his niece. Anything more would be an insult.

* * *

Elinor wakened in the early hours of the next morning when light was filtering with increasing strength through the curtains and illuminating the magnificent unfamiliar room. In that first instant of reason after a very eventful night, she knew only pure terror when she thought of the unknown that faced her.

What the heck had come over her? Complete insanity? It was barely thirty-six hours since they had met and she had spent the night in Prince Jasim's bed, letting him make love to her over and over again. In truth she wasn't sure she would be able to walk if she got out of bed, since he had proved a very demanding and seemingly tireless lover.

She lay watching him in the half-light, dreamily, tenderly admiring the strong classic bones of his profile and the way blue-black stubble enhanced his wide stubborn mouth. While her body might ache from his attentions, familiarity had not bred contempt. He was beautiful. He still took her breath away and that scared her, because she had never believed in love at first sight.

But what else was she to make of the powerful emotions assailing her? He had not been out of her mind for a second since they'd met and she felt remarkably comfortable with images and reflections of him fully occupying her every waking thought. On a horse and in bed he was her every dream come true. Yet she hardly knew him and surely he could only think less of her because of the ease with which she had fallen into his arms?

Content to be the full focus of her admiration, Jasim was wondering if he dared take her one more time. He couldn't get enough of the sweet, tight release of her warm, willing body. But the servants would be up and about soon, and a lifetime in a royal palace had taught him how fast scandal hit the household grapevine and went places one would prefer it did not reach. The deed was done, accomplished in record time too, he savoured with ruthless satisfaction. His brother would never look at her now. Too warm, he sat up and tossed back the duvet and saw the blood stain on the white linen sheet.

'Good morning,' she whispered, looking all shy and flushed and utterly adorable.

Unlike his unlamented Sophia, Elinor *had* been a virgin, Jasim registered in substantial shock. Yet he had taken her with all the finesse of a stallion covering a mare. A virgin: quite a statement for a young woman of twenty-one in a world where casual sex was commonplace. A twinge of rare guilt pierced Jasim; he would never have chosen to seduce a virgin. But even had he known beforehand, would he have left her untouched while he was aware that Murad would have found such purity a mouth-watering temptation? He had now contrived to smash the possibility of a relationship that could well have driven his brother into setting Yaminah aside and replacing her with Elinor as a second wife. For all his extra-marital affairs, Murad was a staunchly traditional man and Jasim was convinced that, had Elinor slept with Murad, his brother would have offered her marriage. Well, at least that disaster could not be enacted now.

Jasim reached for Elinor and pulled her into his arms. 'Good morning,' he husked, cupping her pouting breasts and gently teasing the swollen pink buds that crowned them.

Elinor was very tense. 'I need to go back to my room—'

'One of the servants will bring you clothes and pack for

you,' Jasim intoned, arranging her against the tumbled pillows and letting his tousled dark head swoop down to capture a straining nipple. One more time, he was thinking, just to get him through the day ahead.

Elinor went from being all soft and purring and quivering with response to sudden rigidity. '*Pack*...for me?'

Jasim wished he had taken more thorough advantage of her before he broke that news. He lifted his handsome dark head and met the anxious questions clouding her green eyes. 'You can no longer stay at Woodrow Court.'

'What are you talking about?' Elinor gasped in bewilderment, pulling away from him and yanking the duvet up over breasts that suddenly felt indecently bare.

Jasim released his breath on a slow hiss of impatience. 'Of course you can't stay here now that we have shared a bed. It would be most inappropriate for you to continue caring for my niece.'

Elinor was so shocked by that announcement that she felt the blood drain from her face and leave her pale. 'You mean that having sex with you is grounds for giving me the sack?'

'I wouldn't put it quite as crudely as that.'

Elinor hugged the duvet to her with furious defensive hands, her eyes prickling with stinging tears. She could not credit what he was telling her, or that he could say such offensive things in that smooth low-key style, as though he were merely making polite conversation. 'Then how would you put it?'

'Our relationship will enter another phase,' he drawled, smooth as polished glass and with a decided hint of warning ice in his tone.

Deaf to that loaded hint of icy withdrawal, Elinor stared

straight ahead and worried at her full lower lip with her teeth. 'What sort of a phase?'

'I want you to move to London so that we can see more of each other.'

Now horribly conscious of her nudity below the bedding, Elinor flung him as frozen a look as she could contrive. 'But I like working here. I love looking after Zahrah.'

'It's unfortunate but it can no longer continue. I cannot conduct an affair with you in the presence of my family.'

'Because you're ashamed of your association with me!' Elinor condemned, and she flung herself out of bed in a passion of self-loathing regret and snatched up the towelling robe.

'No, it would be indiscreet and unacceptable behaviour on my part. In London I can do as I like and what I would like is to see more of you,' Jasim declared, brilliant dark eyes welded to her angry bemused face as he willed her to accept the change in her status. 'We can't turn back the clock on our intimacy. You must trust me. Say your good-byes to Zahrah and I will have you out of here by lunch-time.'

Elinor snatched up her discarded swimsuit with a shaking hand. She was in shock and deeply confused. Throughout the night hours he had been the passionate lover of her dreams but, all of a sudden, he was laying down the law and making non-negotiable demands that threatened to tear apart her entire life. 'And if I was to say, no, I'm not going anywhere and let's forget we ever crossed the boundaries?'

'I believe you are too sensible to challenge me.'

This time around she felt the distinct chill in the air and

it raised goosebumps on her exposed skin. His dark gaze was black and cold. For the very first time, she sensed the steel of him, the fierce ruthless purpose that powered him beneath the charisma. The discovery of what lay at the core of him unnerved her. He was determined that she leave Woodrow Court and if that was how strongly he felt, she did not see how she could remain and live in constant fear of her wanton behaviour being exposed. 'I wish I had known what I was getting into,' she breathed starkly.

'You do now,' Jasim pointed out silkily.

Elinor wanted to shout, but she was too shaken by what had happened to let go of her temper until she knew exactly where she stood. In her own heart she was committed to him but she did not like the way he was treating her. What were the chances that a royal prince would treat her with respect? Or come to truly care for her as anything other than a sexual partner? She realised that she had thrown the dice in a game without knowing what she was really playing for and now it was too late to go back and argue about the rules. As long as she could get a reference she would soon get another job in London. Whatever, it seemed she had thoroughly burned her boats at Woodrow Court.

She managed to return to her room, mercifully without running into anyone. She stood in the shower with tears running down her taut cheeks, trying to overcome the suspicion that in sleeping with Jasim she might well have made the biggest mistake of her life. He was turning her life upside down but she wasn't ready yet to give up hope of a better future and walk away. As soon as she was dressed she sought out Zahrah and told the little girl that she had to leave to go and see her family. She hated telling a lie and Zahrah was quite tearful until her beloved nurse took her off for breakfast. Elinor knew her charge would be fine without her. Zahrah's main source of security was the elderly nurse who had always been with her.

She skipped breakfast and packed. A manservant came to the door for her luggage and Jasim called her on the house phone at noon. 'I'll see you in London,' he told her. 'I'm grateful that you're being sensible about this. I couldn't hide our relationship and I don't intend to.'

Strengthened by what felt like a far-reaching pledge of faith on her terms, Elinor got into the car waiting outside for her and it was only then that she marvelled at her failure to demand to know exactly where she was being taken. Mid-afternoon, she preceded her driver into a lift in a tall block of luxury flats. He had not a word of English so she couldn't question him and she wondered as she was shown into an apartment if it was where Jasim lived when he was in the city. Was he moving her in with him? Surely not? She reminded herself that she had a healthy bank account and was far from powerless when it came to looking out for her own best interests. But, even so, the sudden changes had cost her dear; she had a cautious personality and her strong attachment to him added entire layers of complexity that made her feel out of control.

An hour later, Jasim strode through the front door. He hauled her straight into his arms and kissed her as if he was set on reminding her of his power over her. Pink lit her cheeks and butterflies fluttered inside her. Everything, she promised herself as she gazed up into his breathtakingly handsome face, was going to be fine. She just had to give them both a little time and space.

But time, she soon learned, was at premium.

'This evening I'm flying to New York for two weeks,' Jasim imparted with a casualness that made her vulnerable heart sink like a stone. 'That's why I had you brought here. I own this apartment and you'll be comfortable here while I'm abroad.'

'I can afford my own accommodation, although I may not need it for long. Most nanny jobs are live-in and if you can sort out a reference for me, I'll have another job by the time you get back—'

Jasim studied her in wonderment. Unable to believe that she could possibly be serious in her desire to be self-sufficient, he released a slightly harsh laugh. 'There's no need for you to look for another position. Nannies must work hellish hours—how would I ever see you? Don't you understand what I'm offering you?'

Elinor stood there very still and straight-backed and increasingly pale. 'No, I must be incredibly thick because I haven't quite worked out yet what you're offering me…'

His charismatic smile slashed his lean dark visage and he took a measured step forward. 'Naturally, I want to take care of you…'

'No, thanks.' Elinor forced a smile that felt rigid on her tense mouth and mentally willed him not to demean her with some sordid proposition. 'The only man who will ever take *care* of me with my agreement will be my husband. I'm willing to wait for you to come back but I'm not willing to be kept by you. I'm a very independent woman and what I give, I give freely.'

Jasim frowned. 'You make it all sound so serious.'

'What happened between us last night drove a coach and

horses through my life and left pure chaos in its wake,' she reminded him gently, a slender hand resting on the lapel of his pinstripe suit jacket. 'Right now, I don't know whether I'm on my head or my heels. I'll stay for a while because I have nowhere else to go in the short term, but I need to fall back to Planet Earth again so maybe it's good that you'll be away for a while.'

Jasim pulled out his wallet to extract a card. 'My private number,' he told her, presenting her with it as though it was a precious gift—which indeed it was. Many women would have done just about anything to gain access to that direct hotline to him, but his staff guarded his privacy with scrupulous care.

Before he could close the wallet, his thumb brushed over the condom packet slotted into it and his blood ran cold in his veins in a deeply disturbing wake-up call. He realised that in his excitement the evening before he had neglected to use contraception with Elinor. Consternation rolled through him. How could he have made such a serious oversight? Although he was usually very careful, they had shared numerous encounters of unprotected sex during the night. What if he had got her pregnant? He reminded himself that, according to Murad, a woman didn't fall pregnant that easily. Certainly, Yaminah had been most unfortunate in that regard. He thought of all that he had read about 'morning-after pills', but he had too much respect for the gift of new life to persuade a woman into taking that option as a preventative measure. He decided that he could more easily live with hoping for the best. Yet, he knew that an unplanned pregnancy would engulf his life like an avalanche, crush his freedom and suffocate him. He barely stilled a shudder at the threat of such an outcome and thought how ironic it was that what his older brother had longed and prayed for to secure the line to the throne should strike Jasim as an absolute disaster.

Within twenty-four hours of Jasim's departure, Elinor quietly signed up with an agency as a relief nanny and found herself plunged straight back into regular, reasonably well-paid employment. Going from one family to the next and staying only a few days in each household was surprisingly enjoyable and kept her too busy to brood. She knew she wouldn't like dealing with a merry-go-round of change for ever but, just then, the freedom from having to forge new meaningful relationships felt like what she most needed. Every night she returned to the luxurious but anonymous comfort of the apartment and fell asleep within minutes of getting into bed.

Jasim phoned her almost every day. The conversations were curiously impersonal and unsatisfying and only made her feel more insecure. The only information he gave about himself was superficial. He never mentioned the future, or that he was missing her. Her period was due at the end of that first week and when it didn't arrive as expected she tried not to worry. She started to feel that she had been very foolish once she acknowledged that she had no memory of Jasim taking precautions that night at Woodrow Court. Had he falsely assumed that she was taking contraceptive pills as so many women did? How could she have been so dense? When her nerves could stand the waiting game no longer, she bought a pregnancy test. The test was guaranteed to give an accurate result within days of a malfunctioning menstrual cycle, so she made immediate use of it.

The positive result stunned Elinor. Somehow she hadn't really believed that she *could* have conceived; somehow such a development hadn't really seemed possible to her. Now she learned that she was very much mistaken. She was expecting a baby, a real, live little baby. In the space of one wildly reckless night Jasim had contrived to get her pregnant.

That same evening she received an unexpected visitor. The doorbell buzzed and when she addressed the caller through the intercom, it was Prince Murad's voice that answered her. Elinor was appalled by his arrival and would have done just about anything to avoid the humiliation of answering the door and actually having to deal with her former employer. Unfortunately there was no decent way of avoiding the issue.

'May I come in and speak with you?' the older man asked politely.

'Of course.' In the elegant living room, Elinor linked her hands tightly together. 'You must be wondering why I left Woodrow so suddenly—'

'Elinor…let me be frank. I know that this apartment block belongs to my brother,' the prince admitted, his expression grave and concerned. 'I am sorry that you have left my employment and I would rather that it had been for any other reason than this. I had a great affection for your mother and I feel responsible for you as her daughter. You have chosen to take a most ill-advised step.'

Her strained face flamed with colour. 'I know you mean well, but I'm an adult and I'm here of my own free will, Your Highness.'

'Jasim has had many women in his life, Elinor. He cherishes none of them, and he will not marry any woman who has already lived with him.'

Elinor's hands twisted. Confronted by such cruel candour, she felt as if her heart were being ripped out at the seams. 'I'm not looking for marriage—'

'But you deserve better than this tawdry arrangement,' Murad pronounced with an angry wave of dismissal that encompassed their surroundings. A small and portly but still dignified figure, he sighed. 'I loved and respected your mother. I would never have asked her to be my mistress. You must value yourself more. Surely this cannot be the future that you wanted?'

Although it was still only early evening, when Murad left Elinor went to bed and cried. Seeing how she had sunk in the older man's estimation had upset her. But, at the same time, she knew that there was no way that she was prepared to become Jasim's mistress! Apart from anything else, her pregnancy would alter everything, she reasoned wretchedly. When he had carted her off to bed in an excess of lusty passion, conceiving a child with her would have been the very last thing on his mind. How was she likely to react to such a shattering development?

Jasim had returned from New York a day early. Warned by his security team that his brother had visited Elinor, he arrived at the apartment a couple of hours later. Murad's seeking out of Elinor had confirmed his every suspicion about the nature of their relationship and he was angry and full of distrust. Never before had his older sibling sought to interfere in his private life! So what kind of a hold did Elinor have over Murad that he had felt the need to come up to London specifically to confront her?

'Jasim…' Elinor sat up in bed with a start as the overhead light went on. 'I had no idea you were coming back tonight!'

Sheathed in a charcoal grey business suit that was beautifully tailored to fit his lean, tautly muscled physique, he looked spectacular. Deprived of the sight of him for almost two weeks, she couldn't help staring and drinking in every tiny detail of his appearance.

In his turn, Jasim was studying the tumbled bed, questioning why she was in it at barely past eight o'clock and asking himself if his own brother could have shared it with her earlier that evening. Her nose was pink and her eyelids reddened and swollen, making it clear that she had been upset and that she had cried. Fierce anger and disgust filled him. 'Evidently…'

'What's that supposed to mean?' she questioned in bewilderment.

'Did you entertain my brother in that bed as well?'

Her eyes widened in shock at that question. 'That's a horrible thing to ask me—'

'But an even more disgusting thing to have to suspect,' Jasim countered rawly, dark eyes glittering like golden diamonds of derision over her. He strode round to the side of the bed, closed a hand round her arm and tugged her upright to face him without ceremony. *Answer me.*'

'Why? Do you and your brother make a habit of *sharing* women?' Elinor demanded shakily, her outrage threatening to strangle her voice. 'I slept with you so, for that reason, you assume I'm just some slut who would be quite happy to sleep with your brother as well?'

The level of her incredulity cooled Jasim's temper and

sharpened his wits. He registered that he had come within an ace of revealing too much knowledge. He had given her no reason to suspect his motives in pursuing her and if Murad was still chasing after her, it would be unwise to either alienate her or turn her loose.

Deeply wounded by his lack of faith in her, Elinor stared at him in angry reproach. What had happened to the guy who had sworn he wanted to see more of her? He pushed a hand through the black hair on his brow and raked it back in a gesture of frustration. She noticed that his hand wasn't quite steady and registered that he was a great deal more disturbed than he was prepared to show. On the outside he seemed so cool and controlled, but inside he seethed with anger, outrage and passion. Suddenly she believed she understood what was wrong. Evidently, the reverse side of that passion was a jealous, suspicious streak a mile wide. On the balance side, however, when she had challenged him he had backed off, presumably appreciating that his suspicions were ridiculously irrational. She wondered if the behaviour of some other woman had taught him to distrust her sex.

'How did you know your brother came to see me?'

'My security team have been keeping an eye on this apartment.'

Wondering if she was supposed to be flattered that he should consider she required that protection, Elinor nodded and began to pull clean clothes out of the drawers in the cabinet by the bed. 'I'll get dressed. We have to talk.'

Jasim tensed. The idea of further discussion was the sort of womanly threat he avoided like the plague. He would much have preferred joining her in bed. Sex would have released his tension and buried the argument much more effectively than a verbal post-mortem.

Stiff and self-conscious now in his presence, Elinor went into the en-suite bathroom to dress, pulling on the jeans and the T-shirt she had chosen at speed. She wished she had had some warning that he would be returning early, for she would have liked the chance to dress up. Glancing in the mirror, she groaned, convinced that she looked horribly plain with her pink-rimmed eyes and weary pallor. When she re-entered the bedroom, Jasim was standing by the window in the living room. He still looked unrelentingly severe and he swung round, saying flatly, 'What did my brother want with you?'

An uneasy flush warmed her cheeks and she wished she could have been more frank with him about her late mother's relationship with Murad. But, on her first day of employment, the older man had made her promise never to divulge that connection to anyone, for he had feared that the truth would be misinterpreted and would cause them both embarrassment. Since her friend, Louise, had already made seedy insinuations about the same issue, Elinor had decided that Prince Murad had been more astute than she in foreseeing what others might make of the story and she had no intention of being equally frank with anyone else. 'The prince thought that I was making a mistake leaving my job and getting involved with you. He said that he felt responsible for me.'

Jasim's superb bone structure set hard as granite beneath his bronzed skin. Well, that was certainly telling him the lie of the land! Murad had been sufficiently angry to follow her to London and question her current circumstances. Jasim studied her exquisite face and the tumble of Titian curls that were so bright against her creamy skin. He wondered how he had ever deemed that hair unattractive. How had he also failed to appreciate the obvious fact that so beautiful a woman might also have the power to set brother against brother? He was stunned that he had contrived to overlook that obvious angle and it was now too late to redress the balance. Wasn't it? He was outraged that Murad had even dared to approach her, crossing boundaries that Jasim had assumed would be respected. She was *his* now.

Elinor sank down in a leather armchair and straightened her slight shoulders. 'I have something to tell you.' Having breathed in deep, she mustered the strength not to make a theatrical production out of her news. 'I'm pregnant.'

However, her quiet low-pitched admission had the same effect on Jasim as a sudden devastatingly loud clap of thunder. He went very still. His expressive eyes hooded over and his aggressive jaw line clenched hard. His sins, it seemed, had truly come home to roost and the minute she spoke he saw his well-organised life spinning out of control. 'It's my fault,' he acknowledged flatly. 'When we spent the night together I didn't use protection.'

A little less defensive once he assumed the lion's share of the blame for her condition, Elinor released her pent-up breath.

'I deserve to pay the price for this,' Jasim said heavily, his classic profile as grim as his tone of voice.

'The price? There is no price—'

'You're wrong. Either we pay the price, or our child will. If you give birth to a boy he will be an heir to the throne of Quaram, but he can only assume that status if we marry and he is born within wedlock. If he is not, my family will never recognise him.'

'An heir to the throne—would he be….honestly?' Elinor exclaimed in astonishment. *'Marry?'*

'I don't think that we have a choice. As soon as you've had your pregnancy confirmed by a doctor, I have to marry you. I refuse to embarrass my family with a scandal and it is imperative that our child is born legitimate.'

Elinor realised that his decisions were based on a different set of parameters from hers but she was impressed by his willingness to stand by their child and look into the future. 'I could have a little girl.'

'She, too, would be denied her inheritance if she is not born within marriage. The birth of an illegitimate child is still a very serious matter in my country.'

'You're prepared to marry me to stop that happening?' Elinor prompted, because she just couldn't accept that he was prepared to go to such lengths.

'I am. Isn't securing our child's future the most important issue at stake here?'

'But we hardly know each other.' Elinor dealt him a pained glance of shame as she forced out that admission. 'I'm only a nanny…you're a prince.'

'Our child won't care who or what we are as long as we love him…or her,' he responded wryly.

She was touched by that assurance and the thought that had gone into it. He was so responsible and he would make a good father; he was already worrying about what was best for their child. All right, she had eyes in her head and she could see that he wasn't exactly celebrating at the prospect of marrying her, but neither was he thinking of leaving her to deal alone with her pregnancy. 'Do you think we could make a marriage work?' she murmured half under her breath.

'I'm willing to make the effort.' His beautiful dark eyes wandered over her at a leisurely pace and lingered on her soft pink mouth and the ripe pout of her breasts until her face burned and she shifted in her chair. 'I find you very attractive. That's a healthy foundation.'

Elinor knew that, with the smallest encouragement, he would scoop her up and take her back to bed to sate the hunger he made no attempt to hide. Her nipples were tightening and the familiar hollow ache was awakening between her thighs. But she felt too vulnerable to give him that signal. She wanted to be more than the woman who satisfied his sexual needs. But even though she wanted more she knew that she was still prepared to marry him on the practical and unemotional basis that he had outlined. If he was ready to give her his full support, she was willing to do whatever it took to ensure a more secure and happy future for her baby.

'I'll marry you, then,' she told him gruffly.

Jasim almost laughed out loud at the idea that he might have required that confirmation. Of course she was going to marry him and snatch at the chance to live in luxury for the rest of her days! Not for one moment had he doubted that fact. 'I'll make the arrangements. Please don't share our plans with anyone for the moment. We need to keep this a secret if we want to keep the tabloid press out of the picture.'

Jasim retreated back to the doorway. Dark-driven anger was stirring out of the ashes of his shock. He had known that he was dealing with a devious and mercenary young woman, who was willing to encourage a married man's

pursuit to feather her nest. Yet, even armed with that awareness, he too had fallen for her wiles and straight into a
sexual honey-trap refined by the guilt-inducing gift of her
virginity. He had played into her scheming hands as easily
as a testosterone-driven teenager. Elinor Tempest had
simply traded her body to the highest and most available
bidder and the pay-off promised to be *huge* on her terms.
Marriage into the Rais ruling family would reward her
with immense wealth and status and that unhappy truth
galled him.

Her face full of uncertainty, Elinor hovered by the bed.
His beautiful golden gaze was cold as charity and she
flushed. 'Are you leaving?'

'I have work to do,' Jasim delivered curtly. 'I'll be in
touch.'

On the day of the wedding, Elinor was torn in two with in-
decision. She had barely laid eyes on Jasim since the day
she told him she was pregnant. He had personally accompanied her to the office of a gynaecologist in private
practice, who had confirmed her pregnancy. She rather suspected that Jasim had regretted doing so when a well-
dressed lady in the waiting room had recognised him and
begun chattering away to him. Since then, though she had
given up her temping work, he had not visited the apartment again or accompanied her anywhere and they had
communicated only by phone. In every way possible he had
distanced himself from her, retreating behind a smooth,
polite façade that she could not penetrate.

She had fallen crazily in love with a guy who didn't
return her feelings, Elinor conceded wretchedly. Would he

ever love her back? Or did the very fact that he felt he *had* to marry her for the sake of their child mean that she would never, ever inspire him to any warmer emotions? Those were the questions that Elinor struggled to find a fair answer to while she prepared all on her own for what she had once thought would be the happiest day of her life.

Too insecure to purchase the white wedding gown of her dreams and wear it, Elinor made do with a cream lace suit composed of a jacket and a slim skirt that came to just below her knees. None of the romantic frills that most women craved seemed appropriate. Jasim sent a car to collect her and she was ushered into the register office where the civil ceremony was to take place. A limp flower arrangement was the dusty room's only claim to glamour. But her attention zeroed straight in on Jasim, dramatically handsome in a dark suit teamed with a gold silk tie, his bronzed angel face grave and oddly forbidding.

Her tummy flipped with nerves rather than excitement because her bridegroom looked more as though he were attending a funeral. *Give him the option of walking away*, a little voice in her head urged her. 'Could I have a word with you in private?' Elinor enquired tautly.

Jasim detached himself from the company of the two aides flanking him and approached her. 'What is it? We haven't much time.'

'There is no obligation on you to do this. If you don't want to marry me, just walk away now. I won't hold it against you. I won't stop you seeing the baby either,' she whispered frantically. 'Just don't marry me because you feel you have to, because it'll cause us both nothing but unhappiness.'

Jasim dealt her a raw appraisal that warned her that he

was seething with emotion beneath the cool front. 'We have a future together with our child. I cannot walk away from either of you.'

'But I don't want a noble, self-sacrificing hero of a husband,' Elinor declared, even as he turned away from her.

Jasim closed a hand over hers and walked her back with him to where the registrar was standing. 'We haven't got time for this nonsense.'

The ceremony was brief and over with very quickly. A shiny new ring on her wedding finger, Elinor got into a limousine that wafted them back through the busy city streets to a hugely impressive Georgian town house set in a dignified square with a lush garden at its centre. Jasim spent the entire journey on his cell phone, which, Elinor acknowledged bitterly, at least saved him from the challenge of having to chat to her. She wondered how he would manage without it in bed, or even if he ever planned to make physical contact with her again. *I've made a mistake*, she thought fearfully. *I've made a terrible, terrible mistake marrying him and now it's too late to do anything about it!*

'We'll have lunch now,' Jasim murmured, guiding her up the steps of the town house and into a spacious hall hung with beautiful oil paintings. 'Why are you so quiet?'

Elinor almost lost her temper with him there and then, almost told him what a horrible wedding it had been and how she had given him the opportunity to back out and that, if he hadn't taken it, the least he could have done was make the effort to ensure that it was a pleasant occasion! But, conscious that his bodyguards and the housekeeper were hovering, she bit back her ire. 'I suppose I'm just tired.'

'You should lie down for an hour.' Jasim signalled the

housekeeper and she was escorted upstairs to a beautiful bedroom.

Angry tears in her eyes at the ease with which he had dismissed her from his presence, Elinor soon decided that she should go back downstairs and tell Jasim exactly what she thought of the wedding he had put her through. Maintaining a stiff upper lip was unlikely to improve the atmosphere between them, but maybe an argument would, she reasoned in desperation. After all, if he didn't know how she was feeling, how could he make things better? But what if he didn't care enough to even want to make things better? That was her biggest fear.

From the window she saw a limo draw up outside. She frowned when she saw Murad's wife, Yaminah, scrambling out, for it had not escaped her notice that no member of his family had attended their wedding. She left the bedroom and headed for the stairs.

The sound of a shrill, raised, female voice greeted Elinor even before she reached the hall. It was Yaminah and she was ranting in French.

'It's my fault you got involved with the girl…didn't I beg you to show an interest in her so that she would *lose* interest in my husband and pay him no heed?' the older woman cried feverishly. 'Now I've ruined your life! I can't believe what you've done. You didn't even get your father's permission to marry her!'

The deep steady tones of Jasim's rich drawl interposed, 'The King would never have given his permission—'

'Then it's not too late. The marriage can be invalidated,' Yaminah exclaimed. 'It doesn't matter that she's pregnant, that can be hushed up. Pay her off, do whatever you have to do, anything *other* than sacrifice your happiness with this mockery of a marriage!'

Listening to that uniquely revealing dialogue, Elinor felt much as if she were being eviscerated with a knife. Perspiration beading her upper lip, she hurried back to the bedroom and straight into the adjoining bathroom where she was horribly sick. All of a sudden, she was realising what a total idiot she had been not to question why a spectacularly handsome prince would start showing a pronounced interest in *her*. Yaminah had asked him to. Murad's wife had feared that her husband was at risk of being led astray by the nanny and had persuaded her brother-in-law to present himself as an alternative option. Goodness, had they really feared that she might have an affair with a married man as old as Murad? Jasim had been a dazzling success when it came to seduction and too virile for his own good, Elinor conceded painfully. No wonder the complication of a pregnancy had hit him hard! Jasim had never really wanted her at all and even less must he have wanted to marry her.

Elinor freshened up and pressed trembling hands to her damp cheeks. She would do Jasim one last favour: for the benefit of them both she would leave him. There was no true marriage to work at, no future to weave dreams around and clearly no togetherness or mutual passion to retrieve. Their whole relationship from start to finish had been a lie, a big fat fakery, to ensnare her and draw her in. She had been more than a little desperate to believe that he could find her irresistible—even though no other man ever had—and now all she was conscious of was a deeply painful sense of shame and humiliation. What a pushover and a patsy she had been!

She rooted through her luggage, which had been brought up, extracting jewellery, keepsakes, important documentation and a few necessities to keep her clothed until she had time to go shopping. She didn't care about abandoning the rest—indeed her entire being was bent on leaving the town house just as fast as she possibly could. She piled everything she was taking with her into a smaller bag and changed into a more practical outfit of jeans and a jacket.

She yanked off her wedding ring and left it on the dressing table. Instantly she felt better about herself. He was gorgeous, rich and royal, but he had taken her for a cruelly manipulative ride that she would never forget. How naïve and immature she had been to give her trust so easily! A woman needed a man like a fish needed a bicycle, she quoted to herself, because her heart felt as if it were being pounded into pieces inside her. She didn't need him when she had herself to depend on, a willingness to work and a comfortable savings account. She and her baby would get by just fine without him.

Even so, tears dampened her face as she crept through the hall and slid like an eel out the front door with barely a sound. She walked briskly down the street and she didn't once look back. She was already making plans to ensure that even though he looked for her he would find it very difficult to find her again.

CHAPTER FOUR

'ALL right, so he's not there right now,' Alissa conceded grudgingly, lodged at the front window and scanning the pavement opposite for the young man she had noticed earlier. 'But I swear he was out there looking up at this apartment most of the day.'

Lindy, a curvaceous brunette, groaned out loud and rolled her eyes at Elinor. 'We haven't got a boyfriend between us but we've attracted a stalker? We don't have a lot of luck, do we?'

Elinor didn't laugh. Anything out of the ordinary tended to make her tense. She was always a little on her guard. Eighteen months had passed since she had set out to make a new life and preserve her independence by cutting all ties with the old. Kneeling, she bent over Sami, slotting her baby son into a stretchy sleep-suit covered with pictures of toy racing cars. He thought it was a game and continually tried to roll away out of reach. She closed a hand round a chubby ankle to hold him steady.

'Sami…stay still,' she scolded, trying to be stern.

Enormous brown eyes surrounded by black lashes as

long as fly swats danced with mischief. He rolled again. At ten months old, Sami had buckets of charm and a huge amount of personality. He was a fearless extrovert to his fingertips. When life went his way he was all sunny smiles and chuckles, but when it went wrong he seethed with melodrama and sobbed up a heartbreaking storm.

'It's bedtime,' Elinor told the little boy, tenderly hugging him close, revelling in his squirming warmth and cuddliness and the sweet familiar scent of his skin.

She usually kept Sami up quite late in the evenings because he was cared for in a crèche during the day while she worked full time. Every morning when she left him there she felt guilty, and evenings, weekends and holidays revolved exclusively around ensuring that Sami had lots of fun and got all her attention.

'Night, Sami.' Lindy patted his little curly dark head fondly as she moved past Elinor to head into the kitchen. 'Fancy a cup of tea before bed?'

'I'd love one,' Elinor admitted wearily.

'Nighty-night,' Alissa said to Sami, tugging Elinor down onto the arm of the sofa so that she could kiss the little boy's cheek.

Elinor tucked her son into his cot beside her bed. His eyes sparkled and he kicked while she went through their usual bedtime ritual, winding up the music box to play its customary lullaby and tucking his toy lamb in beside him. She read his favourite story, showing him the pictures through the bars of the cot. Slowly Sami wound down, lowering his eyelids until his thick ebony lashes fringed his olive-toned baby cheeks. Content to watch him, Elinor got ready for bed and stayed until he was fast asleep.

'You've let the tea get cold,' Lindy sighed when she emerged.

'I'm used to cold tea.'

Alissa had already retired for the night. Lindy was frowning at Elinor. 'You looked really worried when Alissa mentioned that she thought that guy had been watching the apartment. Did you think it might be Sami's dad? Was he violent?'

Elinor froze and gave her flatmate a shocked look. 'My goodness, no, nothing like that!'

'I couldn't help wondering and I felt I had to ask just in case someone turns up asking for you.' Lindy watched Elinor pale at the idea. 'What *are* you scared of, then?'

If Elinor had not been so accustomed to sidestepping all such questions to conceal her past history she might have weakened and told all. Lindy and Alissa were more than just flatmates. They were true friends, who had stuck by her throughout her pregnancy and done their utmost to be supportive.

'Not violence but…maybe losing custody of Sami,' she confided, finally voicing her deepest fear.

'I don't know what you're worried about. Single mothers outrank single fathers in the custody stakes.'

Elinor shrugged, reluctant to admit that she had married her child's father, although she was pretty sure that the marriage would have since been dissolved. For what reason would Jasim have retained that bond with an unwanted wife, who had vanished on their wedding day? But she was always afraid that he might still be looking for them because she had kept his child from him. And she felt amazingly bad about that sometimes. However, she didn't feel she could trust a man who had done what Jasim had done to her. It was Jasim who had taught her how devious, cruel and cold-blooded he could be. He might have married her, but he hadn't cared about her or even respected her, so how likely was it that he would be happy to share Sami with her? Sami was far too precious to be put at risk.

The following morning, Elinor checked Sami into the workplace crèche that made her daily life so much simpler than it might otherwise have been. The crèche was brand new and state-of-the-art and it was the main reason why Elinor had been overjoyed when she got a job at Havertons. Having passed a year-long business course with flying colours after Sami's birth, she was now happily employed in a position with the company. Indeed there was only one cloud in Elinor's sky. At the start of the month, finding it difficult to negotiate the uncertainties of the financial markets, Havertons had changed hands, swallowed up by a much larger player in the insurance hierarchy. Ever since then office tensions had risen. Everyone was worried that jobs would be shed and Elinor was equally afraid that the new ownership would close the crèche as a cost-cutting measure.

When Elinor arrived at her desk, the buzz in the accounts department was unusually loud. 'What's all the racket about?' she asked her neighbour.

'The CEO of RS Industries is paying us a personal visit today. The big bosses are hyper at only getting a few hours' notice.'

Just over an hour later Elinor was summoned to her manager's office and she was only a little anxious as to the cause.

'Miss Leslie,' Daniel Harper greeted her with a frown, using the surname she had assumed when she'd left Jasim. 'You're to go up to the top floor immediately and present yourself at Executive Reception.'

Elinor looped a straying auburn curl back behind a delicate ear and murmured uncertainly, 'Am I allowed to ask why?'

Daniel sighed. 'You can ask but I can't answer you. Your presence has been requested upstairs and I'm afraid that's all I know about the matter.'

Made uneasy by his perplexity and concerned that somehow she had got into trouble, for she had never before been on the executive floor, Elinor headed for the lift. As she was whirred up several floors she reminded herself that her recent appraisal had rated her well for her diligence. She studied her reflection in the shiny stainless-steel wall, wondering if she should have taken a moment to tidy her hair, for her rebellious curls were always trying to escape confinement. Her calf-length grey skirt and white ruffled blouse were unexciting, but when she had begun putting together an office wardrobe she had found it easiest to ring the changes by sticking to plain base colours.

In the act of walking towards the reception area she centred her attention on the group of men already standing there. She recognised the MD of Havertons first, a tall toothy man with thinning hair and an anxious expression. Only as she drew closer did she recognise the bold classic profile of the even taller male to one side of the MD and her footsteps faltered. Shock washed over her like a drowning tidal wave. Her skin turned clammy and broke out in goose bumps. It was Jasim! Yet she fought the conviction, reasoning that such a coincidence was so unlikely that she *had* to be mistaken.

But when he turned his arrogant dark head in her direction there could no longer be any room for doubt. Her heart started to thump frighteningly fast, adrenalin pumping up her responses as apprehension threatened to overwhelm her. Sheathed in a faultlessly cut black business suit that was the last word in tailored sophistication, Jasim looked spectacularly handsome and stylish. For a split second, Elinor collided with deep-set dark golden eyes that glittered like fire in the impassive planes of his bronzed face. Her throat closed over. Yet, even on edge with stress and trepidation, she could not suppress the leap of her senses in response to his presence. Although she hated him she could not be impervious to his charisma or the simple fact that, from the crown of his proud dark head to the soles of his almost certainly handmade shoes, he was still indisputably the most gorgeous guy she had ever seen in human form.

'Miss Leslie?' The MD addressed her as affably as though they were friends instead of complete strangers. 'I believe you have a child in the crèche here. His Royal Highness, Prince Jasim, the CEO of our parent company, has requested a tour of the crèche facility in your company.'

So determined was Elinor not to betray her nervous tension that she automatically half extended a hand in polite greeting and then let it drop back to her side again as Jasim's stunning eyes smouldered like punitive flames over her. She sensed the anger restrained by his fierce self-discipline and, since she considered herself to be just as much an injured party as he evidently did, she lifted her head high and thrust up her chin in challenge.

Jasim was inflamed by that defiant look in her bright

green eyes. After what she had done, how dared she challenge him? How dared she masquerade under a name that was not hers and stroll up to him without so much as a womanly blush on her cheeks? What a performer she was! A woman without a drop of shame over her conduct, he reflected bitterly, repressing his bitter anger with difficulty, for she had run away with his son and kept him apart from him.

'Miss Leslie,' he breathed in gritty acknowledgement, his veiled gaze scanning her flawless features and lingering for several taut seconds before lowering to the cushioned swell of her full lower lip. His memory of the taste of her sent a current of electrifying erotic intent straight to his groin and he set his teeth together, infuriated by that unruly physical reaction.

An aide already had the lift waiting for them. Elinor stepped in again, her mind a hive of bemused activity. 'CEO of our parent company,' the managing director had said. *Jasim?* Did that mean that his was the visit that had got everyone in such a tizzy? And that he was the new owner of Havertons and also the CEO of RS Industries? And if it did, did that mean he had *accidentally* contrived to take over the company that employed her? Elinor did not believe in ridiculous coincidences. In her opinion if something looked suspicious, it probably was. The silence sizzled with undertones. Her tummy sank like a stone while the lift travelled downward. Sami was surely the only reason that would lead Jasim into professing an interest in seeing the crèche, she reasoned fearfully. He had to know that their son was there…he wanted to see Sami.

'I wasn't expecting our next meeting to happen in a public

place,' Elinor remarked, only recalling the two bulky body-guards occupying the lift with them after she had spoken.

'Be grateful for it,' Jasim breathed with roughened bite.

The raw anger in his hard gaze sent a spooky chill down her taut spinal cord. Even so, Elinor could not resist shrugging a slim shoulder in dismissal of that masculine warning. 'We have nothing to say to each other.'

'On the contrary,' Jasim contradicted icily. 'I have a great deal to say to you.'

Infuriated by his patronising tone of address, Elinor breathed in deep, because while she could easily have matched that assurance she was not looking forward to the inevitable confrontation. He was a rat, a dangerously clever, unfeeling and unscrupulous rat, who had brazenly played on her trust and naivety to get her into bed. Her face burned at the humiliating recollection of what an easy touch she had proved to be. At the same time, however, there was one subject that she felt she had to tackle.

'I was very sorry to hear of your brother's death,' she remarked stiffly, recollecting how shocked and upset she had been to read about Prince Murad's sudden death from a heart attack the previous year.

'We were all shocked. Murad had a health check every few months but nothing irregular was ever identified,' Jasim proffered grimly. 'He was a bitter loss.'

Elinor had felt sad when she had read about the older man's demise and then rather guilty when, soon afterwards, she had gone out and sold the diamond engagement ring she had inherited from her mother, Rose. The eye-watering value of the ring had astonished her and she had used the proceeds to buy the flat she currently shared with her friends. The security of a decent roof over her head had made single parenthood seem less intimidating.

She entered the crèche at a smart pace. The manageress, Olivia, had been pre-warned and was waiting at the entrance for them. Jasim was quick to engage her in well-bred conversation.

Elinor, however, was in panic mode. Spotting Sami re-clining in a baby seat and playing with a brightly coloured toy, Elinor went straight to her son and released his safety belt to lift him. Sami chortled with pleasure and opened his arms wide. Anxious tears prickled the back of Elinor's eyes as her arms closed round his precious weight and warmth.

'Elinor…' Olivia called. 'You can go into my office if you like.'

The older woman's eyes were bright with curiosity. Elinor evaded them, pacing back towards Jasim's tall, darkly handsome figure with extreme reluctance. But he wasn't looking at her. His entire attention was welded to the little boy she held and when she got close he startled her by reaching out. 'Let me hold my son,' he urged with unconcealed impatience.

Elinor saw comprehension fly into Olivia's face, only to unleash an even more avid expression of curiosity. Although she had no desire to let go of Sami, she did not want to risk a scene that might upset her child. And Jasim, she registered as she clashed with his expectant dark eyes, was very likely to fight hard for what he wanted. She waited until she was inside the older woman's office before handing Sami over. Jasim's hand inadvertently brushed her arm and she was so aware of him that she was vaguely sur-prised not to see fingerprints left behind on her skin. Jasim clasped the little boy with care and held him out to examine, keenly scrutinising every inch of Sami's fearless little face. There was a quality of bemusement and wonder in Jasim's stern gaze that unsettled Elinor and made her feel very uncomfortable. Brown eyes sparkling, Sami smiled at Jasim and made no objection when Jasim brought him closer. His father's confident handling made it clear that he was no stranger to young children.

'He is the only boy born in my family for many years,' Jasim said gravely. 'It is a crime that we have been unable to celebrate his birth.'

A…*crime*? Well, that was certainly letting her know how he felt and more than hinted at the weight of blame he intended to foist on her. Resentment stirred like a knife twisting inside her and her soft mouth compressed into a mutinous line. 'If Sami wasn't present, I would tell you exactly how I feel about you—'

Jasim elevated a sardonic ebony brow, for he was astonished by the attack. 'Do you think I am interested in such a dialogue after you walked out on our marriage?'

An involuntary sour laugh fell from Elinor's lips. 'Marriage?' she repeated drily. '*What* marriage? It was as much of a fake and an insult as your supposed interest in m—'

'Meaning?' Jasim queried, angling his handsome head back as Sami sank an inquisitive little hand into his father's luxuriant cropped black hair and yanked hard.

'Sami, stop that…' Elinor instructed, leaning forward to detach Sami's grasping fingers from his father's hair.

'He can do as he likes with me,' Jasim countered squarely.

Elinor slung her child's father a look of flagrant loathing.

'Like you do? Your brother's wife comes to you with some absurd tale of her husband being led astray by the nanny and you leap right in and seduce me to order? Were you proud of the lines you spun me to get me into bed?' she condemned in a voice that was starting to shake with betraying emotion. 'What sort of a *real* man uses a woman like that? How could you sink that low?'

The healthy glow of his complexion had receded while his fabulous bone structure clenched taut. His dark deep set eyes flared bright as flames and he did not back down an inch. 'You eavesdropped on Yaminah that day. She was hysterical. I did wonder if you had overheard something—'

'I wasn't going to stay with you anyway,' Elinor told him vehemently. 'Not with the way you were treating me! I've got more pride than that, pregnant or otherwise, Your Royal Highness, and the last thing I needed was a reluctant liar of a bridegroom!'

'Silence!' Jasim bit out with ferocious disdain, every inch of his rigid bearing telegraphing his outrage at the abuse she was unleashing on him. 'I will not tolerate being spoken to like that!'

In the smouldering silence that stretched, Sami suddenly burst into noisy tears and stretched his little arms out pathetically to Elinor for comfort.

'Now look what you've done!' Elinor shot at Jasim furiously as she summarily snatched her son from his grasp. 'You've frightened him.'

'Your lack of control and manners did that,' Jasim contradicted without hesitation.

'*Manners?*' Elinor gasped. 'You can talk about manners after what you did to me?'

'Enough,' Jasim told her with icy restraint. 'I'll see you at the town house at seven this evening. I'll send a car for you.'

Elinor banded both arms round Sami in a protective gesture as she recognised in dismay that he clearly already knew where she lived. 'Don't bother. I won't come.'

'You're my wife,' Jasim breathed in a low-pitched growl.

Elinor spun away from him over to the window. 'We're still married?' she prompted tightly.

'Of course we are still married.' A lean hand curved to her slim shoulder to turn her back to him. Brilliant dark eyes assailed hers with cool purpose while the achingly familiar scent of his citrus-based cologne drifted into her nostrils. 'And I want my wife and my child back.'

'That's out of the question.' Elinor rested her chin on Sami's fluffy black curls and studied Jasim wide-eyed over her child's head because she didn't understand where he was coming from. Why would he say such a thing? He could only be saying it because he wanted Sami. As the silence deepened his shrewd gaze looked directly into hers.

Her mouth ran dry and her heart rate speeded up. Images of the night they had shared infiltrated her mind. Instantly she relived the feel of his lean, bronzed, perfect body, hot and urgent against hers, and the insatiable need he had roused and then satisfied over and over again. Her cheeks burned as her nipples tingled and lengthened beneath her clothing and a sensation like warm honey flowed between her thighs.

The atmosphere was thick with sensual tension. Jasim was rigid and strenuously resisting a powerful urge to touch her. 'I believe I will also enjoy the wedding night you denied me,' he murmured huskily.

Elinor shut him out by the simple dint of closing her eyes. She was so hot inside her clothes she felt as if she were burning up, but shame that she could be so wanton followed closely in the wake of her body's treacherous responses to him. 'It's not going to happen,' she told him flatly.

Jasim vented an unappreciative laugh and at the sound of it her eyes flew open. 'You're my wife,' he said again, as if that very fact outranked everything else and rendered even her hostility meaningless.

'Hopefully not for much longer,' Elinor traded on the way back into the nursery.

A brooding presence, Jasim watched Elinor tuck Sami back into a baby seat and was then distracted by a nursery assistant while his mother made good her escape.

On the way back to her desk, Elinor was taken aback by the tumult of emotions swamping her and bringing overwrought moisture to her eyes. Dimly she acknowledged that she was very much in shock at Jasim's descent and what it might mean to her and Sami. She had few illusions about the challenge she faced. Jasim was a Crown Prince with friends and contacts in government circles and big business and he enjoyed unlimited wealth and power. He could easily afford to hire top lawyers and launch a custody battle. Whether she liked it or not, she was going to have to share Sami with him.

It was not a compromise she found it easy to even consider, for she hated Jasim bin Hamid al Rais. She had believed herself to be strong and he had made her weak. It was degrading to acknowledge that she could have fallen in love as easily as a daydreaming teenager. But, worst of all, Jasim had cruelly misjudged her moral fibre when he'd given credence to Yaminah's fears that her husband was paying too much attention to the nanny. That was all such ridiculous nonsense, Elinor reflected bitterly. With the exception of their first meeting and their final one at Jasim's apartment, Elinor had never been alone on any other occasion with Prince Murad. Their few conversations had taken place in either his daughter's presence or that of other staff. Nothing said during those brief harmless dialogues had been in any way improper or even mildly flirtatious. Her pride and her principles revolted against the knowledge that Jasim and goodness knew who else had chosen to believe she could be capable of any other kind of behaviour.

But consternation swept away her angry thoughts when she picked up her son at the end of the day. Two bulky bodyguards were now stationed outside the nursery.

Olivia advanced towards Elinor uncomfortably. 'The prince insisted there must be a security presence to watch over his son while he is in our care. He also asked me not to mention their relationship to anyone else. Naturally I'm not going to breathe a word to anyone. I want to keep my job.'

'I'm sure this is just a temporary arrangement,' Elinor declared with more confidence than she felt, particularly when the same men followed her from the nursery and the older one informed her that a car was waiting to take them home. Rather than get involved in a dispute, Elinor acquiesced, but when she finally reached her apartment she was deep in troubled thoughts that were laced with a dangerous urge to simply pull up sticks and flee before Jasim sought to impose any more rules and restrictions.

'My goodness, you're back early,' Alissa commented when she entered the apartment.

And Elinor shocked them both by bursting into floods of tears. She hadn't let herself cry when she'd walked out on her sham of a marriage or during the unhappy aftermath while she struggled to build a new life rather than wallow in pointless regrets and self-pity. She hadn't even let herself cry when she'd given birth to Sami alone. But Jasim had taken her by surprise and all of a sudden and without the slightest warning the world had become an intensely threatening place.

'What on earth has happened? This is not like you at all,' Alissa muttered in dismay just as Lindy came through the front door and demanded to know what was going on.

There and then, Elinor let down her barriers and told the truth about Sami's conception and the secret marriage that had broken her heart and smashed her self-esteem.

'Sami's father is your husband? And a prince? Does that mean Sami is a prince as well?' Alissa enquired in a daze.

'I haven't a clue.' Elinor blew her nose and lifted her head again. 'About the only thing I do know is that I couldn't face going on the run with Sami—it wouldn't be fair to him.'

'Of course, you're not going to do anything daft like that,' Lindy interposed. 'That's only your panic talking.'

'I want a divorce. I assumed that Jasim would already have taken care of that!' Elinor erupted in a helpless surge of resentment over that fact.

'You can discuss that with him tonight,' Lindy replied.

Alissa frowned. 'Shouldn't you at least *try* being married for Sami's sake ? I mean, what was the point of getting married in the first place?'

Elinor paled before that uncompromisingly direct enquiry. 'Everything changed the minute I heard Jasim talking to Yaminah—'

'Basically I think you only really heard Yaminah raving and what she said could well be hogwash,' Lindy commented. 'Anyway, don't you think that the idea that Jasim deliberately set out to seduce you is a bit, well…improbable?'

Alissa nodded quiet agreement with the other woman's assessment. 'You're a very beautiful girl, Elinor. It's more likely that Jasim was simply attracted to you and the relationship was ruined by you falling pregnant when you had had virtually no time together as a couple. So dealing with the pregnancy took centre stage. Whatever you say about Jasim, he was very keen to stand by you and support you.'

Elinor groaned out loud and raked a frustrated hand through the auburn curls on her brow, her green eyes clouded by the growing confusion that had replaced her earlier certainty. 'You two have a totally different take on the whole situation.'

Lindy laughed. 'Of course we do. We're not personally involved and we're being wise after the fact, which is always easier. But I do think Jasim sounds like the sort of guy who might have deserved more of a chance than you were willing to give him.'

Elinor didn't want to hear assurances of that nature, particularly from Lindy, who always saw the best in people and invariably argued on the side of kindness and common sense.

'I also think…' the more shy and less outspoken Alissa ventured, 'that you need to make allowances for the fact that you didn't marry into an ordinary family—'

'Yes,' Lindy chipped in with her agreement. 'They're

fabulously wealthy and royal, and Sami isn't just an ordinary little boy either if he's in the line of accession to the throne. So how can you possibly expect to keep him to yourself?'

After that conversation Elinor had plenty to think about. She was in shock at an unbiased view of events that was very much different from her own. She wondered if she had been guilty of licking her wounds in silence for too long and if, during that process, her decisions had been unduly influenced by her bitterness, hurt and resentment. Had she overreacted on her wedding day? Should she have confronted Jasim there and then?

Those were the questions Elinor was tormenting herself with while she showered and changed. Shortly after she had bathed and fed Sami and left him in Alissa's care for the evening, the car arrived to collect her. Casually and comfortably dressed in black leggings and a colourful purple top that finished mid-thigh, she climbed into the limo and breathed in deep. One way or another she would sort everything out and *without* getting upset. After all, it was eighteen months since their disastrous wedding and it was time she rose above resentment and wounded pride and moved on, she told herself squarely.

CHAPTER FIVE

JASIM, on the other hand, was not in the mood to move on anywhere. The past still had too strong a hold on him and his estranged wife's dismissive approach to him earlier that day had outraged him. He would not have cared to relive the eighteen months of hell that her disappearance had put him through. A male who had long prided himself on his discipline and equanimity, Jasim could not comprehend why he was suddenly suffering from fierce surges of pure caustic rage.

When Elinor walked into the drawing room at the town house, Jasim was immediately struck by only one fact. 'Where is my son?' he demanded.

'I didn't bring Sami. I left him with my flatmate.'

'Didn't it occur to you that I would want to see him again?' The lean bronzed angel's face that had so often haunted her dreams was taut with annoyance. Jasim settled censorious dark eyes on her slender figure. She was dressed like a teenager, he thought impatiently, his attention lingering on the skin-tight leggings that defined her long coltish legs, shapely knees and slim supple thighs and the bright top that revealed the tantalising valley between her high, full breasts. Perfect breasts, he recalled, and his mind was suddenly awash with detailed erotic images, which had a predictable effect on his libido and only contrived to set his temper even more on edge.

Immediately on the defensive and responding to the smouldering atmosphere, Elinor blanked out his tall, powerful presence as much as possible because she hated the reality that she still found him wildly attractive. And, even as she stood there infuriated by his attitude, her mouth was dry and her pulses were quickening in treacherous response to his proximity.

'Why didn't you bring our son?' Jasim pressed.

Elinor bridled at the tone he employed, which suggested that he was dealing with someone rather slow on the uptake. 'There's too much tension between us. I didn't want to plunge Sami into the middle of another argument.'

'I have a nurse here ready to take care of him.'

The fact that Jasim was already thinking ahead to make childcare arrangements on Sami's behalf totally unnerved Elinor and roused her protective instincts. 'I wouldn't want Sami to be with a stranger—'

'Thanks to your selfishness, my entire family and I are strangers to Sami—are we *all* to be excluded from knowing him on that basis?' Jasim slung at her with biting derision.

Elinor did not appreciate being called selfish and she flashed him an accusing look. 'You're the one who created this situation.'

'How so? I made you my wife in good faith.'

'I don't accept that. I heard Yaminah talking,' Elinor reminded him with spirit while she noted the black density of the eyelashes that enhanced his stunning dark golden eyes. 'She got some nonsensical idea in her head that I was after her husband and that he was interested in me. Her suspicions were completely without foundation.'

'When my late brother gave you a ring that was a family heirloom worth a fortune, he made his interest in you *very* clear,' Jasim condemned, a slight tremor rippling through his lean, powerful frame as he recalled his repugnance at that more recent discovery. In his eyes that discovery had delivered a damning indictment of Elinor's morals. Yaminah's fear that she might lose her husband to the nanny had been soundly based in fact, for Murad would never have given a ring from the royal jewellery collection to a woman he only planned to have an affair with.

At his comeback, Elinor's eyes had flown wide in dismay and she swallowed awkwardly. 'How did you find out about that ring?'

'How do you think I finally found you?' Jasim demanded with a sardonic laugh. 'The inside of the ring was stamped with symbols that marked its history and ownership. When you sold it—for a tithe of its true worth—it eventually passed into the hands of a jeweller who recognised its provenance and importance. He contacted our embassy to make discreet enquiries.'

Elinor was stunned that the diamond ring she had sold had ultimately led to her being tracked down. 'Your brother did not give that ring to me personally. He gave it to my mother,' she protested in a rush.

Jasim's ebony brows pleated. 'Your *mother*?' he jibed.

'When my mother was a student, Murad fell in love with

her and asked her to marry him. Your father, however, wouldn't allow it and they broke up. Your brother wouldn't take the ring back.'

Jasim was still frowning, his incredulity palpable. 'If you are telling me the truth, it is not a story that I have ever heard before—'

'Probably because it happened over thirty years ago!' Elinor interrupted without apology. 'But the point is that it *did* happen and a couple of years ago, when he was re-visiting his old college at Oxford, Murad decided to look my mother up again. He had heard that she had married a professor in the history faculty, but not that she had died several years ago.'

'Naturally, I will check this extraordinary story out.' But Jasim remained resolutely unimpressed by the past connection she was suddenly proclaiming between their families. It stuck him as fanciful and unlikely in the extreme.

'Your brother simply turned up at my home and I had to tell him that my mother had passed away. He was very disappointed and sad and I asked him in. When he found out that I was a newly qualified nanny, he urged me to apply for the job of looking after his daughter.'

'Why didn't you share these facts with me before?'

Her gleaming green gaze narrowed, Elinor searched his darkly handsome features, absently admiring his classic bone structure. 'Your brother asked me not to mention the connection to anyone in case it was misinterpreted. And when I met you I had no idea that you were suspicious of what my relationship with him might be. You *did* think he had some sort of inappropriate interest in me when you came to Woodrow, didn't you?'

His brilliant eyes were level and unapologetic and his strong jaw line had an aggressive slant. 'It was possible. In the past Murad had indulged in a series of extra-marital diversions.'

'Well, I wasn't one of them!' Elinor lifted her head high, defying his unimpressed appraisal. 'For goodness' sake, you know you were the first man I slept with!'

Jasim shifted a broad shoulder in a manner of dismissive assent that incensed her.

'What the heck is it going to take for me to convince you that my dealings with your brother were entirely platonic?' she threw at him furiously.

'We are neither of us stupid. A clever ambitious woman would have been careful not to offer intimacy in advance of a more serious and profitable relationship,' Jasim pointed out flatly.

That alternative interpretation of the facts was the last straw for Elinor's temper. Focusing indignant emerald-green eyes on him, she snapped, 'How *dare* you insinuate that I was some gold-digging schemer ready to break up another woman's marriage? I hate you…I can't wait until we get a divorce!'

'You'll have to wait a long time. I have no intention of giving you a divorce,' Jasim informed her stonily. 'I want you to live up to the promises you made when you went through that marriage ceremony with me.'

Elinor folded her arms in a sharply defensive movement. She was livid at the manner in which he was standing in judgement over her while refusing to believe her side of the story. 'No way!' she told him baldly.

Jasim lifted his imperious dark head high and rested his

attention on the ripe curve of her soft pink lips. 'I am prepared to stand by my promises and give you another chance.'

'I don't *want* another chance from you!' she bawled at him, her pride bristling in revolt from that condescending offer. 'Do I strike you as that much of a doormat?'

'Sami needs both of us. He also needs to be living in Quaram where he can learn the language and culture of the people whom he will one day rule. That requirement is not negotiable,' Jasim imparted with steely cool.

Elinor's response to feeling threatened was to go straight into attack and she took an angry step forward. 'I'm not prepared to live abroad and certainly not with you, so we have a major problem. I don't trust you...I don't trust you at all!' she blazed back at him without hesitation.

Jasim closed lean brown fingers round her wrist and tugged her to him. His sardonic dark golden gaze flared down into hers. 'You may not trust me but you still can't take your eyes off me.'

'That's a ridiculous lie—how can you be so vain?' Elinor raged, although a tide of colour had flooded her cheeks and sexual awareness was like a firework flaring through her body, sending a chain reaction through every skin cell. Memory was taking her back and stealing away her resistance; it was a very long time since that night of passion.

He closed an assured hand into the tumble of her Titian curls and tilted her face up to his. Scorching eyes raked over her and she trembled, maddeningly conscious of the tightening of her nipples and the surge of heat and moisture at the apex of her thighs. At an almost scornfully slow pace, he tugged her up against him and traced the fullness of her lower lip with his fingertip. When that finger slid between her parted lips it was the most erotic thing she had ever known and the tightening knot low in her pelvis made her press her thighs together in an effort to contain the tingling sensation of immediate arousal.

The silence sizzled as their eyes collided. He kissed her with smouldering sexual skill and she quivered violently, fighting the tiny ripples of arousal currenting through her body with all her might. His tongue delved deep in a sweeping reconnaissance that tensed her every muscle.

'Am I vain?' Jasim husked against the swollen pink contours of her mouth. 'I don't think so. I excite you.'

And that was the taunt that finally gave her the strength to do what she should have done much sooner and push him away from her. On legs that were distinctly unsteady she stalked over to the window, where she stood struggling to catch her breath. But he had hit her problem right on the head, she acknowledged with bitter self-loathing. *Excitement.* He filled her with it and seduced her with it. She could not resist that wild charge of electrifying excitement or the explosive high ignited by his touch. Even standing there with her hands curled into defensive fists, she could still feel the magnetic pull of him and the painful aftermath of a desire that had to go unsatisfied.

'Have you nothing to say?' Jasim drawled smooth as silk.

Affronted by the knowledge that he knew her weakness, Elinor spun back to face him, a hectic flush staining her delicate cheekbones. 'Sami is much more important to me than excitement!'

'If that is true, I honour you for it, but you should also have the ability to foresee our son's needs both now and in the future,' Jasim asserted. 'As a boy grows he will need a father more and more. All of my family will cherish him, as will I—'

Elinor tore her attention from him. 'I don't want to be your wife.'

'But you *are* and for Sami's sake that must not change. A divorce would create a great scandal in my country and would be a lifelong source of shame and embarrassment for our son.'

At that news, her heart sank inside her. She could feel the bars of a steel cage of restraint tightening round her. If Sami's standing could be damaged by their divorce how could she push for one? Could she be that selfish? Could she think only of what she wanted now at this point in time? Or should she be willing to compromise? From below her feathery lashes she studied Jasim, her gaze wandering over the proud slash of his bold cheekbones, the classic hollows beneath, the arrogant jut of his narrow-bladed nose segueing down into the chiselled perfection of his well-formed mouth. She remembered the silky feel of his hair beneath her fingertips, and, more dangerously, the heat and urgency of his strong lean body against hers. She tensed in rejection.

He was gorgeous and she was married to him, but he was also utterly without conscience and ruthless when it came to getting what he wanted. A chill like an ice cube melting settled low in Elinor's stomach. He wanted Sami…

CHAPTER SIX

THE following afternoon Jasim strode out of the office he had picked to work in for its proximity to the nursery. He paused by the glass barrier to look down into the crèche on the floor below.

Sami was in a high chair just within his father's view, his dark curly head turned towards an assistant, who was serving snacks. Jasim's ebony brows drew together in a frown. His son appeared to spend too much of the day strapped into seats and play equipment like a miniature prisoner in perpetual physical restraint. He was safe but bored, his freedom to explore severely curtailed, and all elements of fun and even learning denied him by such a restrictive care regime.

A troubled light in his keen gaze, Jasim reluctantly recalled his own desolate childhood. He had never known his mother and he had not even been able to put a face to his father until he was over ten years old. Nobody had ever swept Jasim up in a hug when he cried; the guidelines for his upbringing had been exceedingly strict. He had been schooled from an early age at a military academy abroad where he had learned rigid discipline and self-command as well as how to handle the beatings and pranks that the younger boys endured behind the backs of the staff. His father had been a distant royal figure of unimaginable power who had censured his second son at a distance through the medium of an aide whenever school reports had showed Jasim to be anything less than top-notch at any academic subject or sport. Thankfully, Jasim had been born both clever and athletic and he had excelled. Even so, his many achievements had won him neither praise nor affection.

Having suffered such a tough upbringing, Jasim was eager to ensure a very different childhood for his son. In Quaram, Sami would not spend a good part of his day anchored in one place. He would be free to roam with attentive staff in tow to ensure he didn't get hurt. He watched as Sami lifted his toast and then, having knocked his elbow on a toy on the tray, accidentally dropped it again. The bread fell to the floor and Sami strained and strained a short arm to recapture it. Sami looked around then, visibly seeking attention, but no one appeared to notice what had happened. Finally the little boy flung back his curly head and started to cry.

Jasim found himself on the stairs without remembering the decision to go there. Huge fat tears were now rolling down Sami's red cheeks. Never had a baby looked so wretched to Jasim. An assistant gave Sami a toy in an attempt to distract him. Sami flung it away in an expression of hot temper that surprised his father. But the little boy's anger was short-lived. From the foot of the stairs, Jasim saw tears overflowing again from Sami's big brown eyes while tempestuous sobs shook his solid little body. His son was the very picture of misery and nobody was even trying to comfort him. Several children were in need of attention and it was a challenge for the assistants to take care of them all. Jasim could not bear to stand by and do nothing for his son. He was pierced to the heart by the sight of Sami's unhappiness. He strode into the nursery, sidestepped the startled manageress, and headed straight for Sami. It took the matter of a moment to release the sobbing baby from his restraints and hoist him up into his arms. Sami clung to his father and continued to sob inconsolably.

'I am taking my son home early,' Jasim informed the manageress.

He lifted another piece of toast from the plate abandoned nearby and presented Sami with it. The child stopped mid-howl, grasped the bread frantically between his short fingers and began to cram it into his mouth. He behaved as if he'd been brought up in a Stone-Age cave, Jasim reflected in appalled wonderment, his immaculate business suit and even his hair bespattered with crumbs.

Jasim emerged with Sami from the nursery to find his security team and his aides awaiting his next move in frank astonishment. Any kind of hands-on parenting in the Rais masculine bloodline had never, ever featured in the annals of the family. But Jasim, in delighted receipt of Sami's beaming two-toothed gummy smile of gratitude, was experiencing an enlightening high of relief and accomplishment and he was impervious to his shocked and uncomprehending audience.

Elinor worked doggedly through the afternoon, in spite of the fact that she was terrified that she would simply fall asleep over her computer. She had barely slept the night before and had awakened with a headache. It had taken

great motivation to go to work and the doubts that had kept
her awake during the night continued to interfere with her
concentration. She continued to torment herself with questions that she couldn't answer. Did she owe it to Sami to give
her marriage a second chance? Was that the best thing she
could do for her son? Sacrifice her needs and wishes in
favour of his taking his rightful place as an heir to the throne
of Quaram? For how long would Jasim stay in London?

There was little point bewailing what could not be
changed now, she told herself heavily. Jasim was who he
was—as was Sami. But she loved Sami to the very depths
of her soul and feared his father's interference in their
lives. Olivia, thankfully, had kept the secret of Sami's pa-
ternity. A few people had asked Elinor what Prince Jasim
was like and why he had been so keen to view the crèche,
but nobody suspected that Elinor had been selected as
guide for any reason other than that she had a child using
the facility.

At finishing time, Elinor caught the lift down to the
ground floor. She was relieved to see that Jasim's security
guards were no longer stationed outside the crèche. Had
he realised how much comment their presence would cause
once enough people noticed them? Walking through the
door, her eyes automatically scanning the room for Sami,
Elinor stiffened at the look of surprise in Olivia's face.

'What's wrong?' Elinor questioned.

The older woman drew her off to one side. 'The
prince took Sami after lunch. I assumed you knew,' she
admitted worriedly.

'*Took*…him?' Elinor queried, the words slurring together
on a tongue that suddenly felt too clumsy to vocalise words.

'He said he was taking him home.'

Perspiration beading her pale brow and gripped by complete overwhelming panic, Elinor pictured desert sand dunes and the power in her legs gave at the same time as the world around her folded into darkness. For the first time in her life, Elinor fainted. She recovered consciousness to find that she was in a seat with her head pushed down low.

'Take a deep breath,' Olivia was urging her in a stressed undertone. 'Elinor, I assumed it was okay because he's Sami's father.'

'Yes.' Elinor recalled that conversation in the older woman's presence and snatched in a shuddering breath. With all her courage she fought off the nausea and the dread that were making it impossible for her to think normally. Would Jasim just snatch Sami and fly him out to Quaram? She suspected that her estranged husband was heartless enough to stake his claim in an aggressive manner. Possession, after all, was nine-tenths of the law and who knew what the law on child custody was in Quaram? She was willing to bet that it would favour the ruling family rather than a runaway wife.

Somehow in the background people were talking and she struggled to regain her focus. 'Are you feeling any better?' Olivia prompted hopefully. 'The prince has sent a car to collect you.'

Elinor glanced up and saw two of Jasim's security team awaiting her at the door and the sense of relief that swept her then was so immense that she felt weak enough to pass out again. Jasim would scarcely have sent a car for her if he had removed Sami from the country behind her back. But how dared he have taken Sami from the crèche without

telling her? She was outraged by an act that had reduced
her to a state of sick, almost petrified, fear and an even
more terrifying awareness of her own impotence. If Jasim
decided to fight dirty rather than talk, what was she going
to do to hold her own?

Her nerves honed to a fine edge of impatience, Elinor
stalked into the book-lined luxury of Jasim's library where
he greeted her from behind his desk. She noted in some
dismay that Sami wasn't in the room.

'Where's Sami?'

'He's asleep upstairs. I will take you to him—'

'I want to speak to you first.' Elinor wasted no time
being relieved that her son was still safe in London. She
got between Jasim and the door and stared up at him, apprehension and resentment combining in a fiery com-
bustible mix inside her. Indisputably sexy blue-black
stubble was beginning to shadow his strong jaw line and
roughen the skin round his handsome mouth. Tipping her
head back even further, she clashed with the cool topaz
challenge of his level gaze.

'You had no right to remove Sami from the nursery
without my permission!' she condemned forcefully.

Ice chilled his hard dark gaze. 'I am his father. I will act
as I think best. Sami was upset and he was not receiving
the level of care that I would expect. That is why I removed
him from the nursery,' he responded with measured calm.

'You had no right. Have you any idea how I felt when
I found out you'd taken him?' she demanded half an octave
higher. 'I was afraid you'd taken him back to Quaram and
I'd never see him again.'

'Fortunately for you I have more scruples than you have,' Jasim said drily. 'I wouldn't do that to you or Sami.'

'But you should have warned me of your plans.'

'I did try to phone you.'

Elinor dug out her mobile and switched it on, seeing that several missed calls had been logged. Some of her anger ebbed away. He had at least tried to contact her.

But Jasim had not finished with her yet. 'As for seeking your permission, why should I have done? Did you seek my permission when you deprived me of all contact with my child for almost a year?'

Elinor moved restively away from the door, her angry colour dulling as he hit her on her weakest flank. 'That was different. I had good reason for acting as I did then.'

'No, you did *not*,' Jasim countered without hesitation, his assurance in contradicting her like a slap in the face. 'Only if I was an abusive parent would you have had an acceptable excuse for ignoring my parental rights. When you walked out on our marriage on our wedding day, you were thinking only of yourself and how you felt at that moment. I refuse to credit that you considered how that decision would affect our child or me.'

Consternation at the accuracy of his accusations increased Elinor's tension. She had backed away as far as the edge of his desk and she leant back against it now for added support. When she looked at him, however, her anger was like a hard bitter knot inside her. His face still had a devastating beauty that cut through her defences. But, even more disturbingly, Jasim also had the proud demeanour and aloofness of a statue set in bronze. He seemed untouched by events that had torn her apart. His self-containment mocked her emotional turmoil and she hated him for it.

Was there any way of overcoming the sense of humiliation and shame she always felt in his presence? Once she had fallen head over heels in love with him and made no attempt to hide it. She had surrendered her virginity within hours of meeting him and that knowledge still marked her as painfully as a whiplash on tender skin. She had failed her own standards and made a fool of herself and those were truths that replayed constantly in her mind when he was around, reviving unwelcome memories of her weakness.

'How did you expect me to feel after I heard what Yaminah had to say to you on our wedding day?' Elinor demanded fiercely. 'Was I really supposed to swallow my disgust at the way you had taken advantage of me to think about whether or not you would make a good father?'

'I didn't take advantage of you. Clearly you were incapable of judging the most important issues at stake. You are too keen to remind me of my supposed sins while ignoring your own,' Jasim intoned with sardonic cool. 'When you staged your vanishing act you put me in an appalling position with my family. I had to tell my father that I had married you but I was unable to produce my wife.'

'Any woman would have walked out after that ghastly wedding!' Elinor launched at him helplessly. 'You hated every minute of it and you couldn't even be bothered to hide how you felt!'

His dark eyes were cold as black ice. 'I was conscious that I was acting without my father's knowledge and I was ashamed of the fact.'

'I offered you a get-out clause before the ceremony even began,' Elinor reminded him with spirit.

'Empty useless words,' Jasim derided. 'To deny our child the status of legitimate birth would have condemned him to a lifetime in the shadows. He could never have known my family or claimed his rightful place among them. I could not have lived with that option. Presenting my elderly father with our marriage as a fait accompli was a lesser evil but not an act I can take pride in.'

'Of course it would have helped had you simply explained all that to me at the time,' Elinor argued bitterly. 'But you kept me at as much distance as you might have kept a stranger, so I'm not about to apologise for the fact that I had no idea what was going on behind the scenes! You showed no consideration to how I felt and I am never, ever going to forgive you for that!'

Troubled by her continuing defiance on the score of an event that he considered trivial, Jasim surveyed her. Why were women so irrational? A wedding was a wedding; they were still married, still legally husband and wife. Anger had banished her pallor, accentuating the jade-green brilliance of her eyes against her flawless skin. Her tumbled Titian curls were equally vibrant and drew his eyes against his will. His gaze dropped to the dewy pout of her mouth and then to the tantalising swell of the lush breasts that stirred with her ragged breathing. Strong and insistent desire surged with ravenous force through Jasim's lean, powerful length.

'Don't you dare look at me like that!' Elinor warned him, fully aware of the tension building in the atmosphere and the wicked coil of heat already forming low in her pelvis.

'You're my wife,' Jasim drawled. 'And I haven't been with a woman since I was last with you.'

Elinor was stunned by that information, while the intimacy of the declaration cut through the distance she was trying to achieve and made her face burn with hot colour. She had believed that their marriage was a mere formality on his terms and had not expected him to stay faithful during their separation. Indeed she had assumed he would divorce her. While she had struggled with a body made clumsy and weary by the later stages of pregnancy, she had miserably pictured Jasim wining, dining and bedding more sophisticated women, turning their heads with his charisma as he had once turned hers. The knowledge that he had practised celibacy just as she had was, nonetheless, a sudden source of immense satisfaction to Elinor. It would have been quite a challenge for him to rein in that high voltage sex drive of his, she reflected sourly, reluctantly prompted to recall the one night she had spent with him.

'I knew I'd find you,' Jasim intoned in husky addition.

'I'd like to see Sami now,' Elinor said eagerly, desperate to escape the charged atmosphere and the wickedly potent sexual images she was already struggling to wipe from her thoughts. She wondered if that was what she hated most about Jasim: his ability to transform her into a sexual creature, alien to the sensible self that she had long known and depended on. But her body was indifferent to such fine principles and she was painfully aware of the hollow ache at the heart of her and the slick moisture gathering there in a response that she could not seem to suppress.

Engaged in watching the wild fluctuation of colour in her cheeks, Jasim was amused until he wondered if she was faking a show of shy unease to impress him. After all, a husband who appreciated her would be much more easily manipulated than one who saw through her wiles. But his suspicions about her true nature no longer added up as neatly as they had once done. Surely a gold-digger would never have walked out on a marriage to a male as wealthy as he was and stayed away without failing to launch a lucrative alimony claim? Of course, she had had a very valuable diamond ring to sell, but she had not netted sufficient funds from that to enable her to survive without seeking employment. The modest office job she had taken didn't fit his cynical view of her either, he acknowledged, while he questioned how deep her attachment to Sami really ran. Did she really love his son? Or was Sami simply a weapon to be used?

He accompanied her upstairs to a room outside which a nurse sat on a chair ready to instantly respond to the little boy's first cry. Zahrah's needs had been equally well catered for, Elinor remembered. Sami was fast asleep in an abandoned sprawl. Elinor looked down at her sleeping son with a lump forming in her throat. Sami was unaware of the struggle of wills created by his very existence. The very thought of losing him terrified her. In such a short time Sami had become the centre of her world and the very reason she lived. Her eyes stung and she blinked rapidly. Sami, she was convinced, was infinitely more deserving of her love and loyalty than any man would ever be.

'How can we possibly resolve this?' she asked Jasim painfully.

'We have only two options. I take Sami to Quaram alone or you accompany us there as my wife,' Jasim proffered smoothly, a light hand at her spine urging her back towards the stairs again.

'You believe that those are the *only* options I've got?' Elinor exclaimed in a tone of angry rejection as they reached the hall.

A manservant pressed wide the door of the library where Jasim invited Elinor to take a seat. 'Of course, if you chose to remain in London where you could discreetly lead your own life, I would naturally compensate you for giving Sami into my care. You would be a very wealthy woman,' Jasim informed her, determined to test the level of her attachment to their son.

Elinor glowered at him in disbelief. 'You honestly believe that I might be willing to *sell* my son to you?'

'It's your decision and sell is an unnecessarily emotive word,' Jasim replied softly.

'No, it's a word as offensive as your offer. I gave birth to Sami, I brought him into this world purely because I loved and wanted him. I will never give him up to anybody else's care and, believe me, no amount of money will make me change my mind!' Elinor proclaimed heatedly.

Jasim strode forward and closed his hands round hers. 'I am happy to hear that assurance. Naturally Sami needs his mother. You must come to Quaram with me—'

Elinor winced, her brow furrowing as she tried and failed to slide her hands free of his without making a production out of it. 'Does it have to be *with* you? I mean, maybe I could travel out to Quaram and stay somewhere and you could see Sami as often as you liked—'

Jasim frowned. 'I will not even dignify that foolish suggestion with an answer.'

'Well, if I ask foolish things that irritate you, whose fault is that?' Elinor demanded between gritted teeth. 'You're the guy who set out to charm me and who hauled me off to bed where you didn't use protection!'

'Haven't we got beyond the stage of hurling recriminations yet?' Jasim demanded, smouldering dark golden eyes welded to the bewitching vivacity of her lovely face and the inner glow of emotion that she could not hide. 'Let us leave the anger behind and move forward. I live in the present and when I look at Sami I do *not* see a mistake, I see the future of my family—'

'But what about when you look at *me*?' Elinor slung helplessly. 'I'm a mistake who doesn't belong in your world!'

A lean masculine hand curved to her hip to ease her closer. Against her stomach she felt the hard swell of his erection and the insistent strength of his potent masculinity. '*I* think you belong,' he breathed huskily.

'That's just sex!' Elinor proclaimed, so full of emotion and frustration she could almost have burst into tears. Her heart was pounding, her mouth bone-dry.

Jasim pinned her to him in that intimate connection with impatient hands. She trembled, fighting the magnetic draw of him as well as the treacherous weakness of her own body. Stunning topaz eyes held hers and a breathtakingly beautiful smile tilted his beautiful mouth. 'You like sex too, *aziz*.'

Her skin burned beneath that confident pronouncement and she had to still an instinctive protest. She wanted more from him than his body, and even as she surprised herself by thinking that thought she wondered where her hatred had gone and loathed herself more than she had ever loathed him. 'We would need a lot more than that to make a marriage work,' she said tightly.

'Stay with me tonight,' Jasim urged, his breath stirring the vibrant curls on her pale brow. 'Let's make a new beginning.'

All atingle inside and out and with goose bumps marking her skin in response to the strong deep tone of his rich dark drawl, Elinor pulled free of his hold before her self-control wavered and let her down again. Once burned, twice shy, she rhymed inside her head. Sex was not that important to her, sex could *not* be that important to her that just the sound of his voice sent receptive shivers down her spine. 'That's out of the question.'

'I have to fly home within forty-eight hours,' Jasim imparted gravely. 'My father's health is very poor and I can't stay abroad for much longer. I must have your answer quickly.'

The speed with which he had snapped back into businesslike mode had taken Elinor aback. But then what more had she expected from him? Persuading her to accompany him home to Quaram was an easier option for him in the short term than trying to wrest custody of her child from her. Jasim bin Hamid al Rais was very practical and far from averse to manipulating her into doing his bidding. When he had described Sami as the future of his family she had truly understood the strength of the opposition she was facing. Unfortunately, a reluctant husband willing to offer her a new beginning on the basis of a night of rampant sex wasn't a tempting proposition. At least not to a sensible woman with some pride, Elinor affixed to the stream of her feverish thoughts. She might have made a total idiot of herself over Jasim eighteen months ago, but that should not mean that she had to spend the rest of her life paying for that act of bad judgement.

Resolved to fight for what best suited her needs, Elinor squared her slim shoulders. 'You were educated here in England, weren't you?'

His ebony brows elevated. 'Not fully. I began my education here when I was sixteen.'

'I don't want to be your wife any more than I believe you want me to be your wife,' she declared tightly. 'I have every respect for your background, your family and Sami's importance to you, but I intend to raise my son here in England. When he's older he can make his own decision about where he wants to live.'

Jasim's bone structure had set taut below his bronzed skin and his thickly lashed dark eyes were grave and cold. 'That is not an acceptable arrangement. I may have been educated abroad, but I was born a second son and my upbringing was very different from Murad's. Sami is the firstborn and my heir. I cannot allow you to keep him here.'

Her nerves succumbing to the terrible bite of tension in the air, Elinor was trembling. 'I'm not asking you to *allow* anything, I'm telling you that I do not *want* to live in Quaram!'

His hard gaze glittered gold with anger. 'You will not dictate terms to me. I hold diplomatic status here and I could fly Sami back home today without your permission. It was a courtesy to offer you a choice. Sami is vitally important to the succession and the stability of Quaram and I will not rest until I can bring my son back to my country because that is my duty.'

'Are you threatening me?' Elinor questioned fiercely.

'I am insisting that you consider your position and

Sami's future with simple common sense, rather than through some fluffy veil of foolish emotion and selfishness,' Jasim drawled in a raw tone of contempt. 'Sami will not be accepted as a future ruler if he is a stranger to our people. He cannot learn our culture and language at a distance and still expect to understand our ways and belong. If you deny him that experience, you will make him an outsider.'

Reeling from that crack about fluffy, foolish emotion, Elinor folded her arms in a sharp defensive gesture. 'I truly hate you for putting so much pressure on me!'

'I do what must be done,' Jasim countered with sardonic cool. 'You have to face reality. Sami is *not* an ordinary little boy. Some day he too will have to learn that responsibility goes hand in hand with great position and privilege.'

Elinor was anything but grateful for those home truths. She felt that Jasim had cruelly plunged her into an intolerable situation, where either she sacrificed her own needs or her son's. Was her son ever likely to forgive her if she denied him easy access to his father and his heritage? Separating Sami from a parent who would one day be a King could well foster uncertainties and divisions that would make Sami's life more difficult as an adult. How could she possibly act against what might be Sami's best interests?

'I want to go home now with Sami,' she breathed stiltedly.

A few minutes later she watched as Jasim bent to lift Sami from the cot. Although awake, Sami was still drowsy from his nap and his little face took on a cranky look when he registered the strangeness of his surroundings. Jasim was amazingly gentle with the little boy and Sami slumped against him and rested his heavy head down trustingly on his father's shoulder. 'He's getting to know me,' Jasim remarked with satisfaction.

At that same moment Sami stole his thunder by espying his mother and throwing his arms wide in a demonstration of enthusiastic welcome. In spite of her stress level, Elinor managed to smile and give her son a hug, while Jasim told her about the toast that Sami had dropped at the crèche. His very choice of words helped Elinor to appreciate why he had intervened and removed Sami—'I could not stand to see him cry like that.' Elinor realised then that she was getting to know Jasim as well, or at least another side to him that she could not have dreamt existed. When it came to Sami, it seemed Jasim was anything but cold, detached and harshly judgemental. Elinor wondered with some bitterness how it would feel to have the same power her son had to stir Jasim's emotions.

But, in the absence of that emotion, she had to consider what was best for her son. She recognised that, unless she was prepared to go out on a limb and risk damaging Sami's future prospects in his father's country, she did not have a choice to make. Moving to Quaram was a necessity, not another option.

'If there is no other way and it has to be done for Sami's sake, I will agree to live in Quaram,' Elinor breathed in a driven tone as she reached the foot of the elegant staircase.

'That is the right decision and it will not be one which I give you cause to regret,' Jasim asserted softly.

'You know very well that you might as well have turned a gun on me when you warned me that you could easily have flown Sami out of the country today without me!' Elinor snapped, compressing her soft mouth into an indignant line.

Yet Elinor also appreciated that, although Jasim was a ruthless, heartless rat, she still had unresolved feelings for him, feelings composed of maybe fifty per cent resentment and distrust, forty per cent sexual fascination and ten per cent hope for a fairy-tale happy ending in which he fell madly, deeply, hopelessly in love with her. But, as her late mother had taught her to have little faith in happy endings, she wasn't about to hold her breath on that score.

She went home and drew up lists of things she had to do before she could leave London for Quaram and she sat up late discussing events and making plans with her friends. The next morning she quit her job and Jasim insisted on taking Sami and her shopping for clothing more suited to a hot climate. She was startled by the number of outfits he deemed necessary and increasingly perturbed by his evident knowledge of what women liked in the wardrobe department.

'You've had an awful lot of women in your life, haven't you?' she opined, while he calmly selected garments that were displayed by a team of sales personnel for their appraisal and announced that he thought she suited bright colours like green and blue.

'I have a certain amount of experience,' Jasim responded with measured cool. 'But it would not be appropriate for me to discuss that side of my life with you.'

Her fingers curled into talons, her nails marking her palms with sharp little crescents. She hated the idea of him *ever* having been with another woman and felt sick at the concept of him being intimate with anyone else but her. Registering just how confused her emotions were around him, she felt her discomfiture increase. 'I didn't say I wanted to discuss it precisely. But the way you swept me off my feet—*literally*—at Woodrow the first day we met was educational,' she murmured soft and low. 'With hindsight I can see I was dealing with an expert womaniser.'

'You're entitled to your own opinion on that score,' Jasim remarked without heat, refusing to argue the point in public.

While it was true that Jasim had enjoyed many women, he was not ashamed of the fact. His affairs had always been discreet and conducted on candid terms. He had learned that most women were delighted to give him their company and sexual pleasure in return for a glittering social life and expensive gifts. Sex had never been complicated for him, but he was beginning to suspect that sex within marriage might well prove to be his biggest challenge yet. He glanced at Elinor, noting the tension still etched into her delicate profile. In his extensive experience all women loved to be spoiled. Not unnaturally, he had assumed that a major shopping trip would lift her mood and please her.

But the pursuit had failed to work its usual magic. It was slowly dawning on him that he had very little idea what went on inside Elinor's head. She gave him wildly conflicting signals. What was the matter with her? Why did he please her less than he pleased other women, who were enthralled and eager to reciprocate when he expressed an interest? Why was she sitting beside him watching the parade of beautiful designer garments with the expression of a puritan invited to an orgy? Sudden devilment gleamed in his dark deep-set eyes. If that was her attitude, he should meet her expectations head-on...

Frustration was filling Elinor to overflowing. As usual, Jasim had ignored her questions and slammed a door shut in her face and he was raising barriers to keep her at a distance. He didn't want her to know him any better. Evidently her role was to be more Sami's mother than a wife to Sami's father. It was an assumption that was to take a thorough beating at their next port of call—a highly exclusive lingerie boutique filled with tiny frilly pieces of satin, silk and lace that shocked Elinor to her unadventurous core. While she stood frozen with mortification by his side, Jasim examined what was on offer and made generous selections of frivolous items of underwear that Elinor could not even imagine wearing. She was outraged by his nerve. How dared he make such intimate purchases on her behalf?

Temper bubbling up in her like a natural spring, Elinor dealt him a furious appraisal when they were back inside the limousine.

'I wouldn't be seen dead dressed in underwear of that sort!' she snapped at him.

Unholy amusement turned his dark brown gaze to simmering gold chips of enticement in the lean dark lineaments of his handsome face. 'Such lingerie would certainly provide a novel look for your departure from the world…but I would much prefer to see you wear them while you were very much alive and kicking, so that I could show you my appreciation.'

'Never in this lifetime!' Colour ran like a betraying banner as high as Elinor's hairline as she recoiled from that riposte and the hot masculine appraisal that accompanied it. As if he was already imagining her prancing about a bedroom in those minuscule confections of satin and lace, designed to enhance and display the female body for a man's gratification!

Jasim skated a teasing forefinger down over the back of her tautly clenched hand. 'Never is a long time, *aziz*. Who can tell what the future holds?'

Elinor snatched away her hand. 'Certainly nothing of that nature, I assure you!' she rebutted furiously, squirming from the suspicion that he was accustomed to provocative displays in the bedroom and trying to encourage her to make an effort in the same direction.

Blissfully unaware of the tension in the air, Sami tugged off a sock and chuckled while he explored his bare toes. Elinor compressed her lips. Not for worlds would she have admitted that the promise of Jasim's appreciation lit a wicked little flame of longing inside her, while the prospect of dressing down in wispy nothings for his benefit had a decadent allure that carried sudden shocking appeal for her starved senses.

Instead she sensibly concentrated her mind on the packing she still had to do and the wisdom of getting Sami to bed soon to compensate for the early hour of their departure the following morning. Tomorrow she would be arriving in a foreign country and she knew that she would need all her wits about her as well as a good deal of adaptability to handle that challenge...

CHAPTER SEVEN

'YOU wish to know what you should wear to meet my father?' Jasim echoed with a frown of surprise. 'He won't take fright at the sight of your legs, if that's what you mean. There is no dress code, although I would aim at the conservative.'

Elinor vanished back into a small cabin on Jasim's private jet where she had been rifling through a suitcase, and wished she had made her mind up about what to wear before she travelled. Jasim certainly wasn't much help! With a sigh she shook out a blue silk dress and jacket, light enough to keep her cool and plain enough in style to suit any occasion. Sami was fast asleep in his sky cot, all the nonsense drummed out of him after an energetic and noisy hour of play with his father. Elinor was still shaken by the recollection of Jasim, careless of the damage he might be causing to his immaculate and beautifully tailored designer suit, getting down on his knees to play hide-and-seek around the seats in the main cabin with his enthusiastic son. It was obvious to her that Jasim already had a huge wow factor for Sami. Without any encouragement from her they were bonding like mad.

The diamond ring on her wedding finger caught her attention and she stiffened. It was the very ring with which Murad had once proposed to her mother, and which she had recently sold. Jasim had returned the magnificent diamond cluster, together with the wedding ring that he had given her, when she'd boarded the jet, insisting that she start wearing both.

'But why?' she had argued, uncomfortable with the engagement ring's sheer screaming opulence and the unhappy history that related it to her mother in her own mind.

'That ring is always worn by the Crown Prince's bride.'

'Your brother didn't give it to his wife,' Elinor could not resist reminding him.

Jasim gave her a grim look. 'But he *should* have done. It was hers by right.'

'You still don't believe what I told you about my mother and Murad, do you?' Elinor prompted tightly.

'I'm sure my father will confirm the story…if it is true,' Jasim completed in a sceptical tone that set her teeth on edge. 'Your own father neglected to mention it.'

Astonished by that casual comment, Elinor snapped, 'When did you meet my father?'

'Soon after you staged your vanishing act. Naturally I traced your father to see if you had been in touch with him.' Jasim recalled the obsessively tidy house and the absence of a single photograph of Elinor. He had not been impressed by the older man's lack of concern for his only child. 'He promised to contact me if he heard from you.'

'My father would never have acknowledged that his first wife enjoyed a romance with one of his students before their marriage. It always annoyed him, particularly as their marriage wasn't very successful. Did he tell you how stupid I was in the academic stakes?'

Jasim froze. 'No—why would he have done?'

'Because I was a major disappointment in that field.'

'When you disappeared, I was worried sick about your welfare,' Jasim admitted flatly. 'Enquiries were made at all the agencies dealing with nannies—'

'While I was pregnant I took an office skills course as retraining. I thought the hours would suit me better after my baby was born. My flatmates became my friends,' she confided. 'Alissa and Lindy were marvellous.'

'I am grateful that you had their support but had you given me the choice,' Jasim breathed, '*I* would have been there for you.'

As the private jet landed Elinor noticed the crowd of people outside the airport. 'Why are all those people standing outside?'

'Our arrival is quite an event. Sami's existence has been formally announced and it is probably safe to say that he is currently the most popular baby in Quaram,' Jasim shared with an amused smile. 'My brother's death was a great shock to everyone and the continuity of the royal line means a great deal to our people.'

Several rows of smartly dressed soldiers teamed with a military band, as well as a smiling collection of dignitaries, greeted them on their descent from the plane. A stirring musical score backed the formal welcome while just about everyone craned their necks to get a look at the baby in Elinor's arms. Rested from his nap, Sami, his big brown eyes sparkling, was looking around with great interest. From a polite distance and only at an affirmative nod from Jasim, cameras flashed to capture the royal party.

A limousine decorated with flags and ribbons collected them from the runway. Surrounded by police vehicles and preceded by motorcycle outriders, they were wafted from the airport into the city and port of Muscar. Everything was much more contemporary and western than Elinor had somehow expected and she scolded herself for not having done more research on her future home. The wide streets of the city were packed with people waving at the caval-cade as they drove past. Jasim gave her a running commen-tary, directing her attention from the stunning ultra-modern skyscrapers and landscaped green spaces that marked the business district to a conservation area, known as the Old City, where ancient mosques, souks packed with craftsmen and listed buildings were proving a strong draw to the tourist industry.

Soon after he pointed out the main government offices, he added quietly, 'There is the palace.'

The limousine rounded a vast fountain before turning down a huge imposing drive lined with trees. Gardeners were industriously watering the lush lawns. Ahead loomed a vast structure with a very strange-looking wavy roof that was the ultimate in avant-garde design.

'It's…er…very unusual,' Elinor remarked.

'Murad commissioned it and it won several design awards. I think it looks more like a hotel than a home and my father detests it, but this will be our home when we are in Muscar. I still believe that the old palace outside the city could have been successfully renovated.'

A throng of people were waiting outside the imposing

front entrance. Jasim explained that the crowd was composed of the household staff and he took charge of Sami to make it easier for Elinor to get out of the limo. Perspiration beaded her short upper lip at the same moment that she left the coolness of the car. The heat from the sun beat down on her. Within seconds she felt hot and uncomfortable. She was also starting to feel rather overwhelmed by the level of interest and attention and exceedingly nervous about meeting Jasim's father, King Akil. All the women hung over Sami with intense interest and admiration while Jasim translated the appreciative comments. It crossed her mind that Murad would have been less gracious and patient with such humble employees.

It was wonderful to step into the air-conditioned cool and shade of the palace. It was built on a very grand scale: the vast main hallway, walled and floored in pale gleaming marble, would have passed muster at an airport. She lingered below the refreshing blast of the air-conditioning until her silk dress no longer felt as though it was sticking to her skin and she had rediscovered her energy.

Jasim rested questioning dark eyes on her. 'Are you feeling all right?'

'It's incredibly hot out there,' she muttered apologetically, wishing she could retrieve the foolish words almost as soon as she spoke them, for what else could it be but very hot in a desert kingdom in mid-summer?

'It will take time for you to get used to the higher temperatures. Do you want to take a break before you make my father's acquaintance?' Jasim queried.

'No, let's just go ahead now.' Elinor swallowed back the additional words 'and get it over with,' which would have been less than tactful. But she really wasn't looking forward to the coming meeting. She was the pregnant foreign wife Jasim had married behind his father's back, a wife who had then disappeared for well over a year. She could hardly expect King Akil to look on a humble nanny with that history as a worthy match for his only surviving son.

They trekked a long way through the building. Footsteps and voices echoed to create a noisy backwash of sound. Eventually they reached a set of double doors presided over by armed guards. The doors were thrown wide, an announcement made by a hovering manservant, and finally they were ushered into the royal presence.

Elinor was shocked by her first view of Jasim's father, who was resting on an old-fashioned chaise longue that seemed ludicrously out of place against the extreme modernity of his surroundings. White-haired, clad in traditional robes and as thin as a rail, King Akil was much older than she had expected and he looked very frail. Formality ruled as greetings were quietly exchanged and then Jasim broke the ice by carrying Sami over for his grandfather's examination. An immediate smile chased the gravity from the older man's drawn face.

'He is a fine handsome boy with bright eyes,' the King commented approvingly to Elinor in heavily accented English. 'You named him after my great-grandfather as well. You have excellent taste.'

Elinor went pink with pleasure at that unexpected compliment. She had picked her son's name from the potted history of Quaram on the royal website. Sami's much-revered ancestor had been a renowned scholar and diplomatist credited with uniting his country's warring tribes.

She didn't bother to admit that she had also chosen that particular name because it sounded conveniently like an English one—Sam—that she thought suited her child.

With an imperious dip of his head, the King switched back to his own language and engaged his son in dialogue. As the older man spoke at length and with much solemnity, Jasim seemed to become a good deal tenser and his responses sounded a little terse. Indeed Elinor could not help but notice the rise of dark blood to Jasim's cheekbones and the revealing clenching of his lean brown hands and guessed that it was a challenge for him to retain his temper. Momentarily, the discussion or possibly what could have been an unusually polite dispute halted while a servant was summoned to escort Elinor and Sami from the room.

Full of fierce curiosity though she was, Elinor was nonetheless relieved to escape the uptight atmosphere. Even so, having noticed the extreme formality that reigned between father and a son, she was wondering why the relationship between the King and Jasim was so strained. An instant later, she was furious with herself for being so obtuse. Jasim had married her without his father's permission and her behaviour as a runaway wife could hardly have added gloss to her reputation. Most probably *she* was the root cause of the trouble between the two men!

A strikingly attractive young woman in an elegant black and white designer dress was walking towards her. A diamond brooch that Elinor thought was rather flashy for daytime wear glittered at her neckline. She paused to admire Sami.

'Your son is adorable. I am Laila, Jasim's cousin, and I have been asked to help you settle in,' the brunette announced, pearly white teeth glinting between raspberry glossed lips as she smiled. She had a wonderful head of thick black silky hair that curved round her heart-shaped face and fell down to her shoulders. Almond-shaped, slightly tilted brown eyes gave her an exotic quality and the heavy lids lent her face a voluptuous aspect that Elinor thought men would find highly attractive.

'Thank you. This is a rather new environment for me.'

Laila led her down a corridor. 'I imagine it is and you must be *dreading* making so many adjustments.'

Elinor tensed. 'No, I'm not quite that intimidated,' she parried.

'Life in the royal family can be very constrained,' Laila continued with an expressive roll of her eyes. 'When I'm in London I can do whatever I like, but it's different here. The King runs a very tight ship.'

Reluctant to get involved in that sort of conversation with a stranger, Elinor murmured instead, 'Murad's death must have hit your family very hard.'

'Jasim already enjoys more popular support than his older brother. Murad's extravagance offended many and his reputation was poor. You and the little boy are definitely the jewel in Jasim's future crown,' Laila quipped. 'A son at first go and when you were only just married—congratulations! We're all impressed to death.'

'I didn't appreciate how much Sami would mean to Jasim's family.'

'And our entire country. I believe history is about to be made on your behalf,' Laila remarked. 'I hear Sami is to be shown off to the television cameras and you are to be interviewed. Such media access to the royal family is unprecedented.'

Elinor, suddenly feeling much more daunted by her role as Jasim's wife than she was prepared to admit to her companion, said nothing.

'This is the royal nursery. An entire household has been designed around Sami,' Laila explained, crossing the threshold of a large room crammed with toys and baby equipment. Half a dozen servants streamed through other linked doorways to dip their heads very low while at the same time striving to get a first look at the child in Elinor's arms. 'I won't try to introduce you because few of the staff speak English. Let them look after him while I show you where you will be living.'

Elinor swallowed hard at the challenge of having to hand over care of her son.

'Sami will be spoiled rotten by everyone,' Laila told her with a hint of impatience as Elinor lingered in the doorway. 'Next to your husband he's the most important person in the palace.'

'Aren't you forgetting the King?' Elinor commented.

Laila guided her back into the corridor. 'That my uncle has lived this long is a tribute to his strength of character, but his illness is steadily gaining on him and Jasim is already taking on many of his father's responsibilities.'

Elinor was somewhat unnerved by the suggestion than King Akil was living on borrowed time. She had known the older man was ill but not that there was no hope of recovery. The suggestion that Jasim might soon have to assume the huge responsibility of becoming Quaram's next hereditary ruler brought a sober expression to her face and concern to her thoughtful gaze. Laila led her across a lushly planted courtyard to another building. The front door opened immediately and a servant bowed very low and ushered them in.

'This is where you will live with my cousin. It's very private.' Laila issued instructions to the servant in her own language. 'I've ordered refreshments.'

Elinor walked into a beautifully furnished reception room. Two servants hurried in bearing laden trays. Clearly their arrival had been well prepared for in advance. She sank down into a richly upholstered armchair and her only concern was the distance between the building and Sami's nursery. She knew she was going to have to speak to Jasim because she could see no reason why Sami had to be housed separately. Indeed she was already wondering if it was a deliberate attempt to make her son less dependent on her.

'You're very quiet. Are you nervous at the idea of becoming Queen?' Laila questioned in surprise as delicate glass cups of fragrant tea were offered. 'I wouldn't be—I would love every moment of being queen and, of course, if you hadn't caught Jasim's eye, I might well have been!'

It took a few seconds before the meaning of that startling announcement penetrated Elinor's troubled thoughts about her son. Green eyes widening, she frowned at her companion in some discomfiture. 'Were you and Jasim—?'

Laila sipped her tea and laughed without any sign of animosity. 'It was my uncle's dearest wish that we marry. But, like most men of his generation, Jasim preferred to enjoy being single for as long as he possibly could…and then you came along.'

Elinor gave the gorgeous brunette an uneasy glance. 'Yes.'

'And now my hopes are in the dust.' Laila shifted a

shoulder in a fatalistic shrug. 'Unless, of course, you would be willing to *share* your husband?'

The question was voiced so casually that Elinor could only loose a surprised laugh at what she could only assume was a joke. 'I don't think that would be my style, Laila.'

'But some women *do* share their men in the Middle East and quite happily, believe me,' Laila murmured soft and low. 'A virile man will never complain about having more than one wife to meet his needs and he will be less likely to stray.'

Elinor was so shaken by that revealing little speech that she struggled to absorb it, refusing to credit that the other woman could possibly be suggesting what Elinor was believed she was. Deeply uncomfortable and feeling very much out of her depth, she snatched up a tiny cake from the plate in front of her and began to nibble at it to occupy her hands. She tasted nothing because her taste buds seemed to have gone into hibernation.

'Now I've really shocked you. I'm sorry,' Laila groaned, setting down her tea and rising to her feet in a fluid motion. 'But such arrangements have worked very well for many marriages. You're a foreigner. There is so much you will not be able to share with Jasim. You don't even speak our language. Yaminah would not agree to Murad taking a second wife and their marriage began to fail soon afterwards.'

Green eyes gleaming with a feisty light, Elinor lifted her head high. 'I'm afraid I'll have to take that risk, Laila. I'm a firm believer in the value of monogamy. Jasim is off the market and I have no plans to share him with anyone.'

'And yet there are already rumours within the palace that that is the arrangement which Jasim is hoping you will consent to,' the exotic brunette advanced, her assurance not even slightly dented by Elinor's tart response.

'I'm sure I can rely on you to quash those silly rumours,' Elinor countered firmly, having reached the reluctant conclusion that Jasim's beautiful ambitious cousin was as poisonous as a scorpion. As for her suggestion that Jasim was hoping for a polygamous marriage, that had to be nonsense. Nonsense spouted by a jealous little cat, who had had her calculating eye on Jasim for herself! As Laila took her leave, however, Elinor was already recalling a truly ghastly story that she had once read about an Arab wife whose once happy marriage had been destroyed by a husband who had demanded and exercised the right to take other wives.

Alone, she was given a tour of the house by the senior manservant, Zaid, who spoke excellent English. The house was enormous and she was relieved by the discovery that there was ample space in which to set up a nursery for Sami. The interior, however, was as stark and contemporary as any within the main palace building. The floors were marble and occasionally wood. The windows had blinds rather than drapes. There were entertainment systems everywhere and elaborate switches to control the temperature, the lighting, the blinds and the music. Although a dressing room packed with male apparel was witness to the fact that Jasim lived there, there were no photos or anything more personal lying around. In fact the rooms had all the personality of a bland hotel.

Elinor was freshening up when she heard a door slam shut downstairs. Hurriedly drying her hands, she sped to the top of the stairs. 'Jasim!' she called.

Jasim strode out of the drawing room and looked up at her. His lean strong face was set in harsh lines and he took the stairs two at a time. 'My father expects us to go through another wedding,' he told her grittily.

'Oh, dear. Did you tell him how much you would enjoy going through that experience again?'

There was no answering humour in the angry dark eyes that met hers as he drew level. 'It is not a laughing matter. He does not consider the civil ceremony which we underwent without his agreement to be legal. He has already made all the arrangements for a second ceremony here and we have no choice but to go along with his wishes. It is to take place tomorrow.'

'My word, that's quick. Can we retrieve Sami before then?' Elinor asked.

'Why? Where is our son?'

Elinor explained about the nursery situated deep within the palace.

His ebony brows knit together. 'The household is half a century out of date when it comes to babies.' He pressed a bell in the wall and Zaid reappeared to receive the stream of instructions that Jasim aimed at him. The older man nodded eagerly and sped off. Jasim turned back to Elinor. 'From now on, Sami will sleep in the same quarters as his parents.'

Elinor followed him into the bedroom and watched him discard his jacket. His movements were oddly stiff and constrained, lacking in his usual grace. She studied his grim profile, the strain etching angularity into his classic profile. 'Was this wedding idea the reason you argued with your father?'

'It wasn't an argument—it was a mild difference of

opinion,' Jasim contradicted, unbuttoning his shirt. 'My father has made many plans for us. I am not accustomed to having my life organised for me. After the second wedding, we are to spend a month in seclusion while we become accustomed to being husband and wife.'

Elinor blinked. 'I beg your pardon?'

'Your disappearing act has made my father very nervous about the likely longevity of our marriage,' Jasim explained with an audible edge of derision. 'He believes that a divorce between us would be a disaster for the monarchy. He is convinced that our marriage will only last if I now take a long holiday from my responsibilities to spend time with you and our son.'

Surprised and dismayed by his explanation, Elinor found herself staring as he snaked free of his shirt, revealing a sleek brown torso rippling with whipcord muscle and marked by a black triangle of curls across his powerful pectoral muscles. 'Oh…'

Jasim tossed aside the shirt in a gesture of fuming impatience. 'I don't have time for such self-indulgence. My father is very ill. I am doing what I can to lighten the burden of his duties, but if I am not available he will try to do too much. He is not strong enough to survive another heart attack.'

The anger that she could see repeatedly bubbling up in him was making Elinor feel uneasy, and the atmosphere was explosive. 'Wouldn't he listen to your advice?'

'Obstinacy is a family trait.' Jasim had fallen still and outrage lightened his gaze to scornful accusing gold while he studied her. 'While lying appears to be your fatal flaw and I must be honest—I cannot stand the prospect of living with a liar because it means that you cannot be trusted.'

'Lying?' Elinor repeated in complete bewilderment. 'What are you accusing me of lying about?'

'I checked out your stupid story about a romance between Murad and your late mother. My father had not the slightest idea what I was talking about!' Jasim informed her in a savage undertone. 'My brother had never approached him with a request to marry anyone before he agreed to marry Yaminah.'

Elinor was astonished by that statement. 'But that's not possible. I mean, my mother told me about what happened. It was a major event in her life and she had no reason to lie—'

'*You're* the liar,' Jasim fired back at her with harsh emphasis. 'Why can't you just admit the truth? Murad gave *you* that diamond ring because you had a relationship with him!'

'That's absolutely not true!' Elinor hurled back at him.

In the simmering silence, Jasim yanked off his boxers. A lithe, incredibly male figure, his strong, hard body would have drawn any woman's attention. Elinor's cheeks were very pink. Even in the midst of a row, she found his sleek bronzed nudity an impossible distraction.

'If I didn't know for a fact that you were a virgin when I had you first, I would throw you out of the palace!' Jasim growled at her, the blaze of his wrath increasing at her refusal to come clean. 'What sort of a slut accepts a ring of that value from a married man and then, not content with that piece of brazen scheming, jumps into bed with his brother?'

'Don't you dare call me a slut!' Elinor flung at him furiously, stalking into the spacious limestone bathroom in his wake. 'You're the one who made all the running in our relationship, not me!'

Jasim switched on the water in the wet room and stepped beneath the refreshing gush. He was disgusted that she had lied to him and that he had had sufficient faith in her unlikely tale to actually broach the subject with his father. Naturally he had wanted to believe her story, for the truth he was facing now was a good deal less acceptable. His wife was a greedy, deceitful and immoral liar, who had used her sexual allure to manipulate his brother. There was nothing to celebrate in that fact and much to be ashamed of.

Even so, he noted without surprise, there was no hint of shame in Elinor's stance. Glorious red hair framed the pale beauty of her face and her emerald green eyes were bright with umbrage. She was fizzing with impotent rage at his condemnation and the sight in no way cooled his deep abiding anger with her. She had tried to take him for a fool and deserved everything she had coming to her. She needed to understand that it was time to clean up her act. If she did not, she was likely to find life very hard, for he had no intention of tolerating her devious ways.

'Well, you did make the running,' Elinor repeated afresh when he failed to respond.

'You didn't exactly fight me off, did you? Why would you have done?' Jasim derided as he washed. 'I played right into your hands. I was a better bet than Murad because I didn't have a wife. Of course you were willing to sleep with me!'

'I can't believe that you're insulting me like this—'

'No?' Water streaming down his lean bronzed physique, Jasim treated her to a lethal look of contempt. 'My brother was much softer with women than I will ever be.'

'You're supposed to be my husband—are you ever going to behave like one?' Elinor hissed, green eyes livid with anger.

'Not while your dishonesty is still fresh in my memory. I want the whole truth from you now,' Jasim decreed in a tone of steely command. 'How far did your tempting of my brother go? It must have been pretty intense if he gave you that ring.'

'You've got it all wrong and I'm not answering your stupid demeaning questions.' Her breasts heaving as she dragged in a deep breath to sustain her struggling lungs, Elinor glowered at him. 'Nor am I willing to go through some crazy second wedding with you…once was enough!'

'You're in the wrong country to issue a threat like that,' Jasim delivered with chilling bite as he sauntered out of the shower and reached for a towel. 'Place me in that kind of position and I swear I will tell my father about your sordid flirtation with Murad. If I do there will be no wedding and you will find yourself flying back to London alone.'

Elinor was chilled to the marrow by that warning, for she was in no doubt of how ruthless he could be. 'You can't threaten me like that.'

Smouldering dark golden eyes clashed levelly with hers. 'Don't tempt me. In Quaram I can do just about anything I want to do, *aziz*.'

'Does that include taking a second wife?' Elinor demanded with stinging scorn, for in the mood he was in she saw no reason to approach the topic with greater tact.

Jasim froze, his smouldering dark golden eyes narrowing and darkening to view her with questioning censure. 'Is that your idea of a joke?'

'No, not at all. It was your cousin, Laila, who suggested that you might be hoping for an arrangement like that…'

Jasim lifted his damp dark head high, an expression of

incredulous outrage stamped in his lean, darkly handsome features. 'She would not dare. Only you would have the bravado to subject me to such an offensive piece of salacious prejudice. It is more than a century since anyone in Quaram took more than one wife,' he spelt out rawly.

'I am *not* prejudiced!' Elinor shot back at him furiously.

Jasim dealt her an unimpressed look and strode out of the bathroom regally, as though he were not wrapped in a towel. Elinor shot after him, unwilling to let the matter lie, even though his shocked reaction was already beginning to make her suspect that she might have fallen headlong into a nasty little trap that Laila had set for her. Having filled her head with melodramatic drivel, Laila had set her loose to either worry herself sick about Jasim's supposed plans or confront her husband with the issue and deeply offend him.

'What a distasteful thing to say to me,' Jasim breathed, his beautiful dark eyes cold as black ice as he cast aside the towel and went into the dressing room. 'You should be ashamed of taunting me with such a tawdry accusation. I'm dining with my father this evening and I won't see you until tomorrow.'

Elinor folded her arms and compressed her lips. She was still very angry with him for misjudging her, but at the same time she was so worked up and upset that she could as easily have burst into floods of tears as shouted at him. 'Why should I care what you do or where you go?' she demanded mutinously, determined not to show weakness.

'Clearly I need to ask you to watch your manners and to avoid controversial subjects like culture with my relatives tomorrow,' Jasim spelt out flatly. 'Remember your behaviour reflects on both Sami and I.'

'I'll try not to embarrass anyone,' Elinor breathed tightly, mortified to death by that request and reminder.

Frozen to the spot, she stood by the window, only dimly aware that he was dressing in traditional robes similar to those his father had worn. As he strode out of the dressing room she turned to look at him. The white cotton *thoub* he wore below the black gold-trimmed cloak was buttoned, embroidered and immaculate. With his head covered and a double black cord binding the *gutrah* in place, his transformation into a regal desert prince was complete.

Twenty minutes after his father's departure, Sami was returned to Elinor's care accompanied by a gaggle of chattering attendants and a long procession of nursery furniture and toys. He was installed in the big room across the corridor from the master bedroom. Once he had gone down for the night, wonderfully impervious to all the excitement that was centred on him, Elinor accepted the light meal Zaid had had prepared for her.

She felt absolutely wretched. Laila had set out to trip her up and had succeeded beautifully with her booby trap of a reference to Jasim's fictional plans to take another wife. Now Jasim was affronted and convinced she had been making fun of him on the score of a delicate cultural issue. He also thought she was a shameless liar; if his father could not confirm Murad and her mother's romance thirty years earlier, there was nobody else to perform that feat for her. Had the King forgotten his elder son's university romance? Or did he genuinely not know about Murad's youthful relationship with an Englishwoman?

Whatever, Jasim continued to believe that Elinor had wantonly schemed to destroy his brother's marriage and take

Yaminah's place, only to surrender that ambition when a more accessible member of the royal family strode into her firing line. If that was what he thought of her, what sort of a relationship could she possibly have with her son's father...?

CHAPTER EIGHT

AT SOME timeless hour before daybreak, voices wakened Elinor. She had not slept well. Her argument with Jasim had kept on replaying inside her head and she had thought of other words she might have thrown, last words, final words, more cutting words, even the *ultimate* putdown. Having run the gamut of those pointless replays she had finally questioned the sheer level of ongoing anger that was preventing her from finding peace. Now her head was heavy, her body weary and her eyes swollen. She felt awful and could hardly credit that this was her *second* wedding day.

Frowning, she sat up in bed, registering from the dim glow penetrating the curtains at the window that the sun had not yet fully risen. She fumbled for the light by the bed.

'Allow me.' It was Jasim's voice and the unexpectedness of his appearance startled her.

'*Yes?*' Elinor prompted tightly when the lamp flooded the room with light and illuminated his tall figure by the bed. He was no longer wearing robes and he bore little resemblance to his usually immaculately groomed self. He was clad in faded jeans and a T-shirt, his black hair was tousled and he was badly in need of a shave. But it was his brilliant ebony-lashed dark eyes and the strain etched there that captured and held her attention.

He spread lean brown hands in an expressive movement that was remarkably eloquent of his mood. 'I'm sorry for waking you but I couldn't sleep. We parted bitterly, which is not how it should be today of all days,' he breathed tautly. 'I lost my temper. I was rude. I was cruel…'

'Yes…' Elinor could barely breathe that word of confirmation because conflicting feelings were at war inside her. He was so serious and full of guilt that she could not maintain her distance and still hate him. With all her being she wanted to reach out to him at that moment and indeed even as she spoke she stretched out a hand to him.

His lean, stunningly handsome face grave, he immediately closed his hand over hers. 'When I have to picture you flirting with Murad, something twists inside me and I am filled with such anger I cannot hold it in,' he admitted in a driven undertone.

As it dawned on her that it was jealousy and possessiveness he was describing her defences gave and she pulled on the hand holding hers to bring him down on the bed beside her. 'But there wasn't any flirting with Murad… *ever*,' she stressed earnestly. 'Your brother talked to me as if he was my father. He never said anything that couldn't have been said in front of his wife or indeed anyone. He was kind to me but that was all.'

Beautiful dark eyes locked to hers, Jasim exhaled slowly. 'I will try to accept that. It is not that I want to disbelieve your story about your mother…'

'But it was that story that brought me into your family's life in the first place,' Elinor pointed out.

Jasim met her clear green eyes, which bore not a shadow of constraint, and resolved to settle the issue by having it investigated. He knew he should have talked to his brother about Elinor, but he had not been able to make himself take that sensible route to enlightenment and then Murad had died. For the first time, however, Jasim was wondering if he could have totally misunderstood Elinor and Murad's relationship, which he had never had the opportunity to observe for himself.

'Please don't think I'm saying something I shouldn't,' but when you mentioned that Murad had had extra-marital affairs, I realised why his wife travelled with him everywhere he went,' Elinor admitted uncomfortably. 'I may be wrong, but I suspect that your brother's wife was insecure and more likely than most to be jealous and suspicious of her husband's behaviour around other women—'

'You are saying that Yaminah saw something that was not there,' Jasim remarked without expression.

'I remember her staring at me once when she saw Murad and I laughing at something Zahrah had said. She didn't speak any English, which was awkward. I think your brother was fond of me in a mild way because my mother had once meant a great deal to him. Perhaps that was misinterpreted, I don't know. What I do know was that there was never any suggestion of sexual interest in his attitude to me.'

Jasim was still challenged to credit that his womanising brother could have been unreceptive to Elinor's looks and appeal. But he was equally determined not to allow the issue to divide them. 'I too suffer from a suspicious nature when it comes to women,' he confessed, lifting a hand to stroke a forefinger along the alluring pout of her full pink lower lip. 'Three years ago, I was seeing a woman called Sophia who belonged to one of your country's titled families. I thought about marrying her. I believed she was a woman of good character and integrity and then the tabloid press exposed her for what she really was…'

'Oh…' Elinor said tremulously, her mind only half on the conversation as his finger slid into her mouth and she laved it with her tongue, heat blossoming between her thighs while she dizzily met his intent gaze. 'And what was she?'

'She'd been a real party girl, who had dabbled in drugs and had countless affairs. She had also had surgery to restore her long-lost virginity for my benefit,' he advanced with a roughened laugh, his attention sliding against his will to the neckline of her nightgown where the shadowy cleft and the peach smooth slopes of her full, firm breasts were on tantalising display. 'Yet that was of much less importance to me than all the lies she had told and I had swallowed. She had me fooled.'

And Elinor heard the lingering bitterness and hurt pride in that admission and recognised how afraid he was that he might fall into the same trap again. 'But you can't possibly believe that all women are the same,' she whispered, her breath feathering in her throat.

'Right now, I don't know what I believe…or that I care, *aziz.*' The hot blood settling heavily in his groin, Jasim brought his mouth down with a driven groan on hers, his tongue plundering the sweetness from between her readily parted lips with an urgency that made her heart pound like a drum within her ribcage.

Jasim jerked back from her with a look of frustration.

'I can't stay. It's almost dawn and it takes hours to prepare a bride for her wedding.'

Elinor was shocked by a desire to pull him back to her and wish her bridal duties to perdition if it prevented them from being together. As he sprang off the bed she raised an abstracted hand to rub her cheek where his stubble had scratched her. What shook her most was the intensity of her desire for him. He was teaching her things about her own needs that she would never have guessed and that she suspected she might never have known with another man, for Jasim's raw passion had lit a similar passion inside her.

'We'll be together later,' Jasim husked. 'But I'm afraid I need a few minutes of grace before I can be seen in public.'

Colour washed her face as she appreciated that he was lingering by the window while he waited for the visible bulge of his arousal to subside. But that she could affect him that way was a source of pride and satisfaction for her as well. He switched out the light before he left and she sank back into her warm comfortable bed and stretched luxuriantly at the prospect of a day that was now shorn of fear and insecurity.

Elinor was wakened again by a slender girl in her teens. Gamila introduced herself and told Elinor in English that breakfast awaited her.

'Lovely, thanks.' Elinor slid out of bed and slid her arms into the wrap she had left out beside the bed. Her attention rested on the untouched pillow beside hers and an ache, an uncommonly painful ache, stirred inside her. It bothered her that she missed Jasim so much. How could someone she had recently believed she hated have come to matter so much to her?

'Prince Jasim ordered a wide selection of food for you,' the girl added.

'I'd like to see my son first,' Elinor said apologetically.

'It's still very early. The little prince is still asleep,' Gamila explained. 'I went in to see him. He is a beautiful baby.'

A warm smile curved Elinor's mouth. 'I think so too.'

Downstairs she entered a dining room where the table groaned beneath the weight of a vast array of food. Elinor discovered that she was extremely hungry and enjoyed orange juice, cereal and two toasted muffins spread with honey. Even while she was eating the house seemed full of activity, with feet passing up and down the stairs and the chatter of many female voices. There was no sign of Zaid or any other man.

Having eaten, Elinor was escorted back upstairs to have her hair washed. It was conditioned and rinsed several times and then piled into a towel while a bath was run for her. She watched as an aromatic bath potion was swirled through the water and rose petals were scattered on the surface. Settling into the warm fragrant water and relaxing her stiff muscles was the purest of pleasures. It was an effort to get out again and swathe herself in a fleecy towel.

Once her hair was dry, Gamila suggested that she dress in casual clothes to head over to the main palace. There on the second floor she found a full-size beauty parlour awaiting her. She knew what the fashion was and consented reluctantly to a waxing session. It wasn't quite as painful as she had feared but she didn't think it was a procedure she would ever want to volunteer for. She agreed to a massage and lay on a narrow padded table where she was pummelled and rubbed with fragrant oil. Slowly the stress drained out of her body. At some stage she fell asleep and wakened without the slightest idea of where she was or how much time had passed to find that she was being given a manicure and pedicure. Relaxed after that nap, she began to take an interest in the proceedings. Her nails glossily perfect, she sat watching while intricate henna patterns were painted onto her hands and feet. She wondered if Jasim would enjoy that traditional touch and smiled. She was relieved that there was no sign of Laila in the gathering of female attendants because she was not sure that she could have kept the peace.

Sami was brought to her while her hair was being straightened and smoothed. He gave her a huge sloppy kiss and settled into her lap like a homing pigeon, intrigued by the amount of activity around her. Her companions looked on Jasim's son with unreserved adoration and when he got down from her knee to crawl off in exploration he was petted and fussed over. Sami lapped up the attention to the manner born and Elinor found herself wondering how her son had ever managed with only his mother to admire him.

Her make-up was done last and then she was guided into another room to be shown the Western wedding dress, which she was apparently to wear. Astonished, for she had expected to be presented with a traditional Quarami bridal outfit, Elinor stared at the white wedding dress, which glittered as though stars had been sewn into the fine fabric. Thousands of crystals caught and reflected the light. It was a wonderfully romantic dress, and when she had put it on she could only marvel at her image in the mirror: her every wedding-day dream was fully satisfied by the magnificent gown. Her henna decorated hands and feet didn't quite match in style, but she didn't think that mattered as she eased her feet into delicate crystal-studded sandals with high heels. A short veil was attached to a silver coronet of flowers on her head.

A magnificent jewel case was brought to her.

'It is a gift from your bridegroom,' Gamila explained and tangible excitement filled the room when Elinor lifted the lid on a fabulous diamond necklace and drop earrings that quite took her breath away. Oohs and aahs of admiration sounded all around her. The necklace was the perfect complement to the boat-shaped neckline of her gown.

With her companions laughing and chattering she travelled down in a lift to the ground floor. When she stepped out a bouquet of white roses was handed to her by a giggling little girl. Moments later she saw Jasim, dressed in a snazzy grey morning suit that was a perfect tailored fit to his tall, well-built frame. She collided with brilliant dark eyes and her tummy flipped and her heartbeat thundered in her ears. The instant she saw him a helpless surge of relief and pleasure engulfed her.

You look amazing. He didn't say it; his mouth framed the words in silent appreciation and she lip-read them with an inner glow of happiness that she could not suppress. She had so many questions that she wanted to ask him. Where had the fairy-tale dress come from at such short notice? Why had he given her the diamonds? Why all the fuss when she had dimly expected a short ceremony? But there was no opportunity for her to speak to Jasim in private. They were ushered into a room crowded with guests and married all over again. Throughout the ceremony, an interpreter stood by her elbow carefully translating every solemn word that was spoken. They exchanged rings. Her ring, at least, was not new and when it was returned to her finger it somehow felt more right on her finger than it had before. The formalities over, she posed with her hand resting lightly on Jasim's arm for several ceremonial photographs.

'Where did my dress come from?' she whispered.

'Italy. I called in favours and described what I wanted for you. It was flown in this morning.'

'I love it. And the diamonds?'

'A traditional gift from the groom.'

A pair of antique sedan chairs was brought in and they were each assisted into them. There was a lot of laughter. Hoisted high, the bride and groom were carried to a flower-bedecked room for the wedding party. Jasim helped Elinor out and her attendants hurried forward to rearrange the folds of her dress. Then, the bride and groom stood at the head of the room to greet their guests. Elinor was astonished when she espied her father working his way through the crush towards her.

A tall bearded man with grey hair and spectacles, Ernest Tempest clasped his daughter's hand and frowned. 'Jasim insisted that I come. Your stepmother couldn't make it. She can't stand the heat in places like this. Well, you've done very well for yourself,' he pronounced. 'Who would ever have thought it? I never thought you'd amount to anything.'

It was over two years since Elinor had last seen her father and he had not altered one little bit. She was amazed that, even with Jasim's encouragement, he had chosen to fly out to Quaram to attend her wedding. Evidently she had her marriage to a royal to thank for that feat.

'I'm really pleased you were able to come,' she said pleasantly. 'Are you staying for long?'

'A few days. There are a couple of very interesting archaeological sites in the north of the country and your husband's organised a tour guide for me,' the older man explained. 'Quite a forceful, managing sort of a chap, isn't he?'

Elinor tried not to laugh at that description of Jasim as her father took himself and his opinions very seriously. 'Yes, he is.'

That rather impersonal dialogue complete, Elinor's father moved off again. In a daze she turned to Jasim. 'I certainly wasn't expecting to see my father here.'

'He's the only family you have, but I would never have pressed him to attend if I had known he was likely to tell you that he thought you would never amount to anything,' Jasim admitted, his annoyance on her behalf heartening. 'I wanted our wedding to be special in every way this time.'

Impressed by that statement and the kind of temperament that prompted healing rather than divisive moves, Elinor would have liked to discuss it further with him. It was at that inopportune moment that Laila, sheathed in an azure-blue evening gown that showed off her fabulous curves, glided up. Tossing a brazen smile in Elinor's direction, the beautiful brunette engaged Jasim in a low-pitched conversation. He laughed a couple of times. The friendly familiarity of their relationship was obvious and it set Elinor's teeth on edge.

'You get on very well with your cousin,' Elinor commented when Laila had finally moved on after a lengthy show of reluctance and many heartfelt sighs.

'We grew up together,' Jasim parried lazily. 'She hopes

you'll forgive her for the joke she had at your expense yesterday.'

'The sharing-you-with-a-second-wife joke in extremely bad taste!' Elinor remarked acidly, indignant at the manner in which the other woman had smoothly contrived to excuse her behaviour.

'Laila has always loved to tease and let's face it—you seem to have been a very easy mark,' Jasim informed her with rueful amusement. 'Do you always believe everything people tell you? No matter how ridiculous it might be?'

Hot-cheeked, Elinor had to bite her tongue to rein back a tart and resentful response. She knew she had been credulous and the mortification of it still stung painfully. 'You took it equally seriously last night,' she reminded him drily.

Jasim inclined his proud head in acknowledgement of that reminder and they sat down side by side in throne-like seats while a meal was served.

'Is it true that your father wanted you to marry Laila?' Elinor could not resist asking in a feverish undertone. 'Did you *think* about it?'

'Of course I did. In many ways she would have been perfect, but I was only twenty-six at the time and although she is very attractive I didn't want to marry anyone,' Jasim fielded.

Perfect and *very attractive* were the words that lingered on Elinor's mind. No, she definitely could not kid herself that Jasim was blind to his cousin's charms. It was an un-welcome reminder that Jasim had only chosen her as his wife because she had conceived his child. While she agonised over that fact the celebration trundled on. Speeches were made, songs were sung and poems of inordinate length about great battles and tragic love were recited. Arabic music was played and several traditional dances, which included a lot of waving of swords and cracking of whips, were performed. As evening fell they went out onto a balcony to watch an amazing firework display.

In the middle of it, Jasim closed a hand over hers and tugged her through a door into another reception room, which was empty. 'We will leave now…' he breathed, one hand lifting to nudge a stray auburn strand of hair back from her soft cheek, his fingers lingering to stroke the delicate ear lobe stretched by the weight of a diamond earring. 'You're the perfect height for me,' he murmured lazily.

She looked up into smouldering dark golden eyes and her breath convulsed in her throat while her anticipation climbed ever higher. He reached for her with purposeful hands and crushed her slender, yielding length to his lean, hard body. The fiery passion with which he drove his sensual mouth down hard on hers thrilled her to death, while the erotic dance of his tongue inside her sensitive mouth made her quiver. Even through their clothing she could feel the insistent swell of his arousal. He shuddered against her, hot and eager with desire, and at the very core of her body she melted with liquid heat.

'You're treating me so differently today—why?' she prompted breathlessly.

'I offered you a new beginning and failed to deliver. That wasn't fair to you or Sami,' Jasim conceded tautly. 'I don't want to sabotage our marriage before it even gets off the ground. Sometimes I can be my own worst enemy.'

'And mine,' she completed unevenly.

'Not any more.' He escorted her out to the lift, assuring

her that her luggage was already on board the helicopter awaiting them.

'What about Sami?' she asked anxiously.

'He will join us first thing tomorrow—'

'Why can't he come with us now?'

'My father has asked that Sami and I do not use the same mode of transport in case there is an accident,' Jasim explained wryly. 'It will be inconvenient for us but I can see the wisdom in his request.'

Her skin went clammy at the mere mention of an accident although she knew they happened every day. She thought it was understandable that Murad's unexpected death should have made the King more nervous.

'Did you enjoy the day?' Jasim pressed.

'Very much,' she said truthfully, her mouth still tingling from the exhilarating pressure of his. 'I was surprised by how westernised it all was though.'

'Western-style weddings are currently the height of fashion in Quaram. I pushed the boundaries further by requesting a mixed-sex party afterwards,' Jasim admitted as he urged her outdoors into the balmy heat of evening. 'My father witnessed the ceremony but the party would have been a step too far for him and he conserves his strength as best he can.'

In the powerful lights that lit up the waiting helicopter, Jasim scooped her up into his arms. The full skirts of her gown foamed up round her slim body as he put her on board. 'You haven't even told me where you're taking me!' she exclaimed in the midst of her laughter.

'A villa on the Persian Gulf that used to belong to Murad. Yaminah asked me to take all her Quarami property off her hands because she has moved back to France to be near her family.'

'How are she and Zahrah managing?' Elinor enquired.

'Rather better than anyone expected. I understand that Yaminah has already acquired an admirer, a former friend from her youth, and Zahrah has always been very attached to her maternal grandparents.'

'Life goes on,' Elinor quipped, cheered by the idea that the older woman might find happiness again.

'Ours has barely begun, *aziz*.' As the noise of the propellers drowned out any prospect of further conversation, Elinor met Jasim's dazzling golden-as-topaz eyes, gloriously fringed by black lashes, and her heart skipped an entire beat.

Suddenly, exasperated by the level of her response to him she closed her hands tightly together on her lap and urged herself to use her head. Jasim had dropped the aggro and made peace with her for a very good reason: he didn't want a divorce. His elderly father had no doubt decided to accept his foreign daughter-in-law for much the same reason. Sami lay at the very heart of her acceptance as a wife and it would be foolish to overlook that reality. Jasim might still suspect that she had attempted to lure his brother away from his wife—and that she'd accepted a very valuable ring in the process—but from now on, he would probably keep his reservations on that score to himself. Why? For the sake of their marriage and the image of the monarchy in a small country, where such matters were still of vital importance.

So, Elinor reflected, it was time for her to jump off the bridal bandwagon that had given her starry eyes and recon-

nect with the ground. What was it about Jasim that could make her behave so foolishly? Last night's insane attack of insecurity after Laila's jibes about his taking a second wife? It had not been her intellect that spawned her reaction, but the tumultuous emotions that Jasim still aroused in her. He had the power to make her jealous and possessive, to lift her to passion and drop her into the depths of despair. The day she had walked away from him she had almost drowned in that sense of despair, until she had picked herself up and focused on her baby rather than her broken heart. If she didn't want to be badly hurt again, she needed to regain that emotional control and distance, because Jasim was never likely to give her the love that she secretly craved from him, was he?

The leader of a large contingent of security staff met them off the helicopter. The villa was a palatial, ultra-modern structure embellished by a verandah, extensive grounds and every possible interior extravagance. 'The views in daylight are spectacular,' Jasim told her, and then he swept her up into his arms to carry her over the threshold.

'You don't have to do fake stuff like this to impress me or make me happy,' Elinor told him uncomfortably. 'I know and accept that this is a very practical marriage. I've got no illusions.'

'It's not fake,' Jasim protested, lowering her down the hard length of his muscular body to lead her upstairs.

'I don't want to get into another…er…difference of opinion with you,' Elinor selected, borrowing his terminology, 'but you never really wanted me. You didn't *choose* me. You were only interested in the first place because you thought that your brother—'

Jasim rested a brown forefinger against her parted lips in a silencing gesture that stilled her tongue. 'Don't go back over that ground again, particularly if you're about to make another set of wrong assumptions,' he instructed. 'This is our wedding night.'

'I know,' Elinor reminded him dolefully, moving into a lamplit bedroom adorned with an over-generous number of flower arrangements. 'But facts are facts—'

'You are a very stubborn woman,' Jasim intoned. 'But we are two different people. Your facts are not my facts. How could they be?'

Blinking warily, Elinor looked back up at his bronzed features, her senses singing against her will at his dark, sleek perfection. His stunning dark golden eyes were sombre and serious. 'How do your facts differ from mine?'

'The first time I saw you, even though I was prejudiced against you and you had been drinking, I still thought you were the most gorgeous woman I had ever seen,' Jasim breathed in a driven undertone of urgency that suggested that practising such candour was still a challenge for him. 'Although I have never found redheads attractive, I really love your hair.'

In tune with that unexpected confession, Jasim meshed long fingers into the tumbled, scented depths of her luxuriant mane. 'I love your hair,' he said again, knuckles brushing her cheekbone, her lips and the curve of her breasts to emphasise the point he was determined to make. 'Your face, your mouth, your very beautiful body. I wanted you as soon as I saw you and with a powerful desire beyond any I have ever known before. That reaction had nothing whatsoever to do with anything I had been told about you…it was private and personal to me and concerns only you—'

Elinor was gripped by the edge of fierce urgency in his dark, level drawl. 'If that's true, I—'

'You must accept that it is true. You must also understand that that reaction was not at all welcome to me,' Jasim stated with a frown. 'Naturally I didn't want to be that attracted to you.'

Elinor had gone from feeling like the consolation prize in the wedding lottery to the most desirable of women. On that issue, at least, his sincerity was highly persuasive, right down to the assurance that he had never previously found red hair pleasing. Her slim shoulders lifted a little, her spine straightening. Her hands sliding up to his broad shoulders, she began to help him out of his jacket.

A surprised laugh fell from his lips. He shrugged off the jacket, dealt with his tie and smiled down at her while she undid the buttons on his dress shirt with unsteady hands. 'You know what you want,' he murmured thickly.

And she knew she wanted him; for the first time in well over a year, she wanted him without any sense of guilt or shame. She knew now, and without any shadow of a doubt, that he genuinely wanted her too. It was a simple truth but an immensely important one for her peace of mind. She parted the edges of his shirt and ran her palms down slowly over the warm, hair-roughened wall of his muscular torso, delighting in the heat and masculinity of him. His breathing quickened audibly when her fingers dipped below his waist. He took her hand and pressed it against the hard contours of his surging erection.

'This will be a night of unforgettable pleasure,' Jasim

promised huskily and he turned her firmly round and began to unfasten her gown.

Pink spots of colour adorning her cheekbones, Elinor stepped out of the rucked-up folds of her beautiful dress. She had never felt more exposed than she did then, with her slender body clad only in the ivory satin underpinnings of her bra, panties and lace-topped stockings.

'I have never seen anything more exquisite,' Jasim swore, studying her with scorching golden eyes of deep appreciation.

A slow burn started in her pelvis as he undid her bra and slid it off.

'You have the most wonderful breasts, *aziz*.'

He moulded his hands to the full firm globes, catching the swollen stiff nipples between his fingers and then backing her down onto the bed to put his mouth there instead. The feel of his lips and his tongue on her sensitised flesh fanned the slow burn at the heart of her into a blaze of tingling heat. He tormented the tender buds until her hips were arching off the bed. Stepping back from her, he shed the remainder of his clothing.

Elinor could hardly breathe for desire and the joy of looking at him. There was a pagan glory to his lean, hard body and his rampant arousal. He pulled her down onto the white linen sheets with him. Her tapering fingers skimmed like butterflies over a powerful hair-roughened thigh. Newly confident, she was touching him as she had long yearned to touch him and the very intimacy of her erotic exploration and her pronounced awareness of how she was affecting him stimulated her even more.

A tremor ran through his big frame and he murmured her name. Her fingertips found him, traced his towering potency and practised a delicious friction before her lips engulfed the most sensitive part of all. She elicited a groan from him and then a protest.

'That's enough,' he told her thickly, lean fingers plunging into her hair as he gazed wonderingly down at her. 'I want to make love to you.'

'And do you always have to have top billing?' Elinor whispered playfully, prepared to stop the sensual torment only in the knowledge that she had him all to herself for a month. And, by royal command, she thought with satisfaction. It was only now when she was starting to appreciate how much Jasim respected his father that she understood how much courage it must have taken for him to marry her without the ailing King's approval.

A wolfish grin slashed his beautiful mouth and he hauled her up to him to kiss her with a fierce, wild thoroughness that answered the hot surge of blood through her own body. Her heart pounded as he arranged her back against the pillows.

'I want you to remember our wedding night for ever,' he murmured silkily.

And much, much later, she knew she would never forget it. He began at her feet and she discovered that places that had never previously been erogenous zones had surprising possibilities, not one of which he overlooked in his devotion to detail. By the time that her heart was racing and every inch of her was damp and wildly sensitive to the skilled caress of his mouth and his hands, she knew her honeymoon was going be a sensual delight from start to finish because he seemed to take so much pleasure from her eager response.

Her entire skin surface was tingling, her straining nipples moist from his attention when he finally deigned to touch her where she was most desperate to be touched. He commented on the waxing that had left her bare and sensitised and she was so excited by that stage that she couldn't even find her voice. Her excitement was growing and growing at an uncontrollable rate. He parted the plump swollen lips that were slick and moist and she gasped out loud, squirming and rocking against him in frustration for more. The hollow ache between her thighs had become unbearable.

'Jasim…*now*!' she pleaded.

He closed his hands to her ankles and tipped them back and took her willing body with all the urgency, strength and passion she yearned for. He plunged hard and deep into her tender core and waves of intense pleasure claimed her with his every thrust. It was gloriously passionate and primal and exactly what she needed. When contractions were rippling through her he groaned as her body tightened round him. She cried out when the explosive ecstasy of climax engulfed her and held him tight while he shuddered and reached his own shattering release in her arms. There were tears in her eyes in the aftermath and a new willingness to face her deepest emotions. She was still crazy about him, she acknowledged. Love had bitten her deep and there was no longer any hope of her escaping its bonds.

Elinor pressed her lips to a smooth brown shoulder, drinking in the warm familiar scent of his skin with intense appreciation and a sleepy smile of contentment. 'Being married definitely has its compensations,' she told him with satisfaction…

CHAPTER NINE

'WERE you in love with Sophia?' Elinor asked, tossing out the question in haste before she could lose her nerve.

Jasim dealt her a look of consternation, as well he might have done at that sudden intimate question. Previously they had been discussing his recent decision in a boundary dispute causing trouble between local Bedouin tribesmen.

Mortified by her own lack of diplomacy, Elinor went pink. 'I'm just curious,' she told him as lightly as she could manage and she was lying through her teeth. In truth she wanted to know every tiny detail of every relationship he had ever had with a woman, which was more than a little sad in her own estimation and likely to leave her disappointed since Jasim was not given to chatting freely about such things.

The early morning silence was broken only by the crunching footfall of their horses' hooves in the sand. They often went riding at dawn when Elinor found the heat easiest to handle. The sun had risen and the peach and pink splendour of the skies was colouring the sand to shades of ochre and red. The arid landscape of stony plains broken by rocky outcrops and vast sloping dunes had become familiar to her, as had the surprising number of animals and the wide range of fauna that survived there.

'Why do you want to know?' Jasim enquired.

Primed to find significance in his every word and hesitation, Elinor said instantly, 'So, obviously you *did* think you were in love with Sophia—'

'No, I did not—'

'But you were thinking of *marrying* her!' Elinor exclaimed in disbelief.

'I was not brought up to regard love as a necessary component of marriage,' Jasim imparted grudgingly. 'She was beautiful, elegant, well educated and spoke several languages. I saw those as important qualities.'

Elinor turned shocked eyes on him. 'I can't believe how cold-blooded you can be!'

'I am not cold-blooded, but love can cause a lot of grief,' Jasim declared in what she could see she was supposed to accept as the closing argument of the discussion. 'A wise man chooses a wife with more than love on his mind.'

'My goodness,' Elinor sighed heavily. 'You'd never have picked me in a million years!'

'But I'm delighted with you now that I've got you, *habibti.*' With those irreverent words, Jasim sent her a wicked slanting grin that made her heart hammer hard inside her. It was a grin that, like his laughter, she was becoming increasingly familiar with and it transformed his invariably serious demeanour. Three weeks of privacy at the villa had given them the chance to discover a lot about each other and had laid a firm foundation for a much deeper relationship than she had ever hoped to have with him.

'Did your parents have an arranged marriage?' she

asked with a frown as she struggled to understand his outlook, which was so very different from hers.

His dark gaze narrowed, his whole face freezing, and then he swiftly looked away, murmuring in a taut response, 'No, but my father's first marriage to Murad's mother was arranged and it was happy, as well as lasting almost thirty years.'

'You know,' Elinor commented in a tone of discovery, while wondering why on earth her question should have created so much tension, 'you never ever mention your own mother.'

Jasim vented his breath in a pent-up hiss of impatience. 'And you are only just noticing? It is considered bad taste to mention her. She ran off with another man when I was a baby and I don't think my father has ever recovered from the disgrace of her desertion.'

Elinor blinked in shock and then shut her eyes in mute discomfiture. The unevenness of his usual quiet, steady drawl told her what an emotive subject she had stumbled on and also how very unaccustomed he was to having to make such an explanation. She said nothing just then. She could only imagine how horrific a scandal must have been caused by his mother's behaviour in so old-fashioned a society. She had seen Jasim's shame as he told her and compassion stirred in her that he should still feel so strongly about something that had happened so long ago, particularly when it was an event he could have had no influence over. But that new knowledge added another telling dimension to her awareness that he found it hard to trust women. At the same time her mind overflowed with questions that she was too tactful to ask him to answer.

'I believe my father is considering another visit today,' Jasim imparted. 'His interest in Sami is heartening.'

'Yes.' Elinor, however, did not find it that easy to sit on the sidelines of those visits. The King and Jasim walked on verbal eggshells in each other's presence and extreme politeness ruled until Sami did something silly and broke the ice. She had often wondered and never dared to ask why the older man and his second son treated each other like strangers.

'I've been surprised by the amount of interest my father has taken in Sami,' Jasim shared with the abruptness of a male striving to reward her with a confidence in gratitude for her not having pursued the more controversial topic of his mother.

'I think your father is trying to get to know you better as well,' Elinor admitted.

'Nonsense…why would he do that?' Jasim countered with distinct derision.

Elinor counted to ten and said nothing. From the corner of her eye she noted that Jasim was still regarding her with expectancy. Having cut off her opinion at the knees, he still wanted to know what had made her think that his father might be trying to mend fences with him. Amused, she held her peace. She still found it extraordinary that Jasim was so volatile beneath that sober, serious exterior of his.

Beneath the safe surface, he had an explosive temper and he seethed with dark, deep emotion. At some stage, however, he had learned to suppress those feelings and make self-discipline and duty his twin gods to be obeyed. Sometimes she marvelled at how controlled he was, rarely showing emotion except in unguarded moments or when he thought he was unobserved. She had first seen the cracks in his smooth outer surface when he played with Sami.

His love and pride for their son shone out. With Sami, Jasim relaxed, and when he played with their little boy he discarded his reserve and dignity. Sami was very much an energetic boys' boy and he made a beeline for Jasim whenever he saw him. In fact every time Elinor saw her child in his father's arms she knew that she had made the right decision when she had decided to give her marriage another chance. Sami adored his father.

And Elinor had come to appreciate that she adored Jasim too, although she was a little more critical than Sami was. But there was no denying that the love she had once refused to acknowledge now ruled inside her, for Jasim had made a great deal of effort to ensure that she was amazingly happy. The guy who was waited on hand and foot, and whose staff revered him for his interest in their more humble lives, brought her breakfast in bed almost every morning. Her eyes sparkled. Once he had fed her to restore her energy he often got back into bed as well. No complaints there, she thought, getting a little breathless just stealing a glance at her handsome husband.

While they had been sent to the villa for privacy, daily flights came in carrying government ministers and courtiers. Jasim was consulted about just about everything that happened in Quaram. She had once read that a man could be judged by the company he kept and, in Jasim, she saw the evidence of that. His opinions were held in high regard, his gravity admired, and everyone was delighted that he now had a wife and child.

'But what must people think about us after that wedding when we already had a baby?' Elinor had asked anxiously during their first week at the villa.

'They think that I married you without my father's permission and kept quiet about you until it was safe to bring you out into the open after Murad's death. While disrespect towards a father is a serious matter, the romance of forbidden love, a secret marriage abroad and a baby son win that contest hands down,' Jasim had explained with unhidden amusement. 'Our second wedding here in Quaram was regarded as a sign of my father's approval and acceptance.'

Since their arrival, he had taken her on several trips into the desert where they had enjoyed the hospitality of the local tribesmen in villages and in goatskin tents. He was very well informed and often in demand to settle disputes. He could sit hour after hour with the tribal elders and listen patiently to arguments, such as what was the correct compensation to be paid for a goat that had strayed into a herb garden, and still give the matter his full attention. She had sat in the back of the tent with the women and children drinking strong sweet tea while a television running off a car battery supplied the entertainment. In the process she had also become hopelessly addicted to a madly melodramatic Quarami soap full of sobbing women, swashbuckling men and disaster.

One evening it had rained and he had taken her out the next day to see the amazing sheets of beautiful wild flowers that had come up overnight on the sand. Her pale skin burned easily in the sun and he was assiduous in ensuring that she was slathered in sunscreen and covered up when the light fell on her. She felt safe with him, cared for, appreciated, she acknowledged reflectively as she dismounted from her horse at the stables.

'I should have told you about my mother before this,'

Jasim admitted without warning over breakfast. 'It is easier for you to hear such a story from me than to embarrass someone else with questions.'

'It's not that unusual a story, though,' Elinor told him gently.

'It is in Quaram, particularly in the history of my family.' Lean, strong face taut, Jasim frowned. 'My father was a widower in his fifties when he met her. She was the daughter of a Swiss doctor and half his age. He fell in love with her and married her very quickly. By the time I was born two years later, I understand the relationship was already under strain as she disliked the restricted life she led here.'

Elinor stopped eating to listen. 'And then?'

'She met another man when she was visiting her family. There was an affair which my father discovered and she fled, leaving me behind. She married her lover. I never had any contact with her.'

Elinor frowned. 'Did you ever *try* to have contact?'

'No, nor did she ever try to contact me. She married several times, had no more children and died a few years ago. I don't think she had a maternal streak. I had no cause to thank her for anything other than the gift of life,' Jasim proffered. 'My father couldn't bear to look at me—the son of the woman who had humiliated him in the eyes of our whole country. He sent me off to a military school abroad as soon as he could.'

'That was cruel!'

'He once told me that he was concerned that I might have inherited my mother's moral weakness. Some years later, however, I learned the *true* reason why my father rejected me. He feared I might not be his child and I was

DNA-tested without my knowledge as soon as the tests first became available.'

Elinor shook her head, distressed by what she was finding out about his disturbed and unhappy childhood. 'How could he be so blind? You look so like him.'

'A physical likeness was not enough to satisfy a man tortured by his suspicions.'

'He punished you for your mother's desertion!' she proclaimed with angry heat.

Jasim shrugged a broad shoulder in a dismissive gesture. 'If that is what he did, it was not deliberate for he is not a vengeful man. I was the unfortunate casualty of a broken marriage and his bitterness. No one has the power to remake the past.'

But that afternoon when King Akil arrived for his third visit, Elinor was convinced that Jasim's father was finally trying to bridge that difficult past with his only surviving son. Unfortunately the older man was too proud and Jasim too accustomed to maintaining formal relations for any advance to be easily made. Elinor remained troubled by the awareness that Jasim had been denied the love and affection of both his parents as well as being exiled to a foreign school as a child to toughen up. She saw the proof of his sad upbringing in the warm affection he continually poured on their son. She was now also wondering if he had ever been in love with any woman or if, indeed, he had the smallest idea of what that kind of love would feel like. Certainly there was nothing in his past experience likely to encourage him to trust a woman enough to love her. Jasim, Elinor recognised then, was likely to prove a long-term project in the love stakes.

In the heat of the afternoon, Elinor often lay down for a nap. She was undressing when Jasim strolled into the bedroom. As he came to a halt, dark golden eyes openly engaged in appreciating the picture she made in a turquoise satin bra and knickers, she went pink.

'I was about to invite you for a swim,' Jasim husked, moving closer and turning her round to fold her back against his long powerful body in a confident movement. 'But you might burn in the water and I would prefer to burn you with the fire of my passion in here.'

He eased her rounded breasts free of the satin cups and stroked the straining pink nipples between his fingers. A tiny clenching sensation in her groin made her gasp, feel the race of arousal flame through her while he brushed her hair off the nape of her neck to press his mouth there. She quivered, arching her spine and moaning as his clever fingers teased the tender skin between her thighs. His touch burned through the taut, damp fabric stretched there and with a sound of impatience he stripped the knickers off, bracing her against the side of the bed and parting her legs.

Trembling with wanton eagerness, she heard him unzip his jeans and waited. He drove into her hot wet sheath with molten urgency and an earthy groan of deep satisfaction.

'You are perfect for me, *aziz*,' he told her hungrily, his hands taking advantage of her position to knead her lush nipples and torment the tiny sensitive bud below her mound.

The surge of her excitement was intense. He ravished her with sensual force. Melting ripples of explosive pleasure seized a hold of her and she cried out at the height of her climax at the strength and wonder of that glorious rush of ecstasy. In the aftermath he dragged her shaking weak body onto the bed with him and held her close, pressing his mouth gently to hers.

'That was incredible,' she framed unevenly.

Jasim smiled lazily down at her. 'It always is with you.'

Releasing her to vault off the bed, he dug into the pocket of his jeans and presented her with a little box.

Propping herself up on one elbow, she opened it to reveal a glittering emerald ring. 'My goodness…it's exquisite.'

'It reminded me of your eyes, *aziz*.' Jasim slid it onto her finger. 'We must make the most of our last week here. I will be very busy when I return.'

She admired her ring. He had dropped his guard, shared his secrets with her. She wanted to tell him she loved him but worried that it might make him feel uncomfortable and her feel something less when he could not return the words. The silence stretched and she curved back into his arms, seeking the warmth and familiarity of him as a reassurance.

On the final day of their honeymoon, Jasim, who had spent odd hours going through his late brother's papers in his study, filled a box with documents and some rare old leather-bound books that more properly belonged in the palace library. Two helicopters sat outside in readiness for their return to Muscar. One of the pilots was ill and in bed in the staff quarters, but it was not a problem because Jasim was a pilot after training for several years with his country's air force.

'I'll be with you in a couple of hours when we have landed,' Jasim vowed as Elinor hovered anxiously. 'Stop looking so worried. I'm qualified to fly fighter jets.'

Elinor nodded agreement and wondered if she was turning into an awful clingy woman who had got too attached and couldn't bear her husband out of her sight. She boarded her helicopter. Smiling at Sami, who was kicking his feet in excitement in his seat, she did up her belt. As the unwieldy craft rose into the air she saw a hurrying manservant bump into one of the gardeners and drop the box he was carrying.

In the act of striding past to get into the other aircraft, Jasim was quick to notice the photograph that had fallen out of one of the books and he bent to scoop it up. It was a faded picture of his older brother as a young man with a woman in an evening gown. She was blonde and small with a wide sweet smile that had a strong tug of familiarity for him. He reached for the book and pulled out the folded sheet of paper also protruding from its pages. It was a letter. The harsh light of the sun at noon illuminating the still crisp copperplate English script, he began to read and it wasn't very long before Jasim was being rocked by an appalling sense of guilt…

CHAPTER TEN

'YOU MUST BE BORED witless after spending a month at the beach, hemmed in by the sea on one side and the desert on the other!' Laila opined, all smiles and pleasantries as she sauntered into the sitting room where her mother, Mouna, was drinking tea with Elinor.

'Laila,' her gentle mother scolded. 'That was impolite.'

Laila rolled unconcerned eyes. 'There are no shops at the beach and Englishwomen are said to be very fond of shopping.'

'But all Englishwomen are not the same,' Elinor responded as she stretched out a hand to restrain Sami from climbing into a large plant pot. 'I like fashion but I get bored trailing round shops. I enjoyed the desert as well.'

'Ninety-nine per cent of women would enjoy the desert with Jasim in tow,' Laila remarked, lowering her voice to prevent her mother from hearing that sally.

Lifting a drowsy Sami onto her lap, Elinor gave the beautiful brunette a serene smile. 'You're probably right. He made a wonderful guide.'

'I hear you have been invited to open the new hotel and leisure complex and that the King has agreed.'

Rocking Sami, who was tired and getting cross, Elinor concealed her surprise at what was news to her and simply inclined her head to the brunette in acknowledgement. Until Laila appeared, uninvited and looking quite ravishing in a white shift dress that hugged every curve, Elinor had been hoping Jasim would get back. Then, aware that the other woman would linger to take advantage of his presence, she had wished Laila away. Now turning a discreet eye to the watch on her wrist for about the fourth time, Elinor was more concerned that Jasim was so late and wondered what was holding him up.

'Perhaps you're about to become the figurehead for our new media-savvy modern monarchy,' Laila commented, with an envy she could not hide, just as an older man in a business suit knocked on the sitting room door.

'Your Highness,' he greeted Elinor, who was still striving to adapt to her new title. 'The King wants to speak to you.'

Totally taken aback by that announcement, Elinor scrambled to her feet clutching Sami. Zaid, always a step ahead in questions of what was required within the household, had already summoned the baby's nurse and the young woman hurried in to take charge of the little boy.

On the way to see the King Elinor was a bundle of nerves, for she could not think of anything that Jasim's father might have to discuss with her and her companion was as unresponsive as a block of wood to her curious questions. Could it be about the opening of the new leisure complex that Laila had mentioned? She would have expected any such request to be passed on to her by Jasim. Almost inevitably she began to wonder if she had done or said something wrong and if his father could be taking advantage of his son's absence to tell her about it.

The King was sitting in the ornate reception room where he conducted most of his meetings. The instant Elinor laid eyes on his stony face and grey pallor, her heart gave a sick thud inside her and she forgot the protocol she had learned from Jasim and spoke first. 'What's happened?'

With his hand he urged her to make use of the chair that had been set beside his. Her legs feeling wobbly, Elinor sank down heavily, her eyes glued to the older man's deeply troubled face.

'Jasim has had to make an emergency landing and the rescue services are trying to locate the site as we speak,' he said in a low fierce voice.

Elinor felt the blood drain from her shattered face and her stomach gave a sick somersault. A horrible jumble of frightening images filled her mind. 'Did he crash?' she asked in a wobbly voice.

'We don't know—only that the helicopter developed a fault. He is an accomplished pilot. He passed out top of his year from the military school,' the older man informed her heavily. 'He will know what to do.'

'He'll be all right…he *has* to be,' Elinor mumbled shakily, terror threatening her desperate attempt to maintain her composure. Had she been alone, she knew she would have crumbled and sobbed out her fear.

The older man was sitting with lowered head and closed eyes, his lips moving as though he was praying.

'He is not answering his cell phone,' he revealed.

Elinor stopped breathing. Jasim had boasted that there was not a corner of Quaram that did not enjoy good network coverage and she knew he never went anywhere without his phone. She stared into space while the seconds ticked by and she prayed harder than she had ever prayed in her life before. Now when she had found such happiness with Jasim, she could not bear to imagine life without him. She heard the buzz of voices beyond the doors and realised that word of the accident was spreading inexorably through the palace; a crowd of people was gathering in the hall. The voices grew louder until she heard the slap of running feet against the marble floor. One of the doors opened with noisy abruptness.

Two of the King's aides erupted into the room closely followed by a couple of Jasim's. They raced down the room and burst into animated speech. Elinor had not a clue what they were saying but was convinced they could not be delivering bad news with so much animation and excitement.

'Jasim has been located,' his father announced grittily, reaching out to grip her hand in a supportive move. 'He is well.'

'*How*…well?' Elinor demanded helplessly.

'Scratches, bruises, but he is whole in limb and he will soon be here with us,' the King proclaimed tremulously, waving both hands in urgent dismissal of his hovering aides, who were staring at him and then swiftly averting their eyes from their elderly ruler.

Elinor turned worried eyes to Jasim's father. Unashamed tears of relief were streaming down the older man's face. He looked at her with anguished eyes of regret. 'He was always good and worthy of praise and I ignored him.'

'It's not too late to change that,' she murmured feelingly. 'It's never too late.'

They sat there together in a surprisingly companionable silence while they waited for Jasim's return. A curious calm had descended over Elinor. She was thinking that she too would have had regrets had Jasim been taken from her without warning. He might have died without knowing that she loved him and that awareness distressed her.

The palace guard in the grounds discharged their guns in long noisy bursts to announce Jasim's return. The King hurried down the long room to the doors to await his son. Elinor had already decided to leave the two men alone to talk, but she needed to see Jasim in the flesh to fully believe that he was safe and unharmed. He strode in, black hair tousled and dusty, the sleeve of his shirt missing and a bandage on his arm.

'I thought you weren't hurt!' she exclaimed in dismay.

'It's only a scratch,' he barked, an expression of shock and incredulity crossing his lean dark features as his father suddenly wrapped both arms round him and enveloped him in a hearty emotional hug.

Although it hurt Elinor to walk away when she too longed for that physical contact to vent her relief from intense fear and concern, she slipped out of the door behind Jasim and left him in peace with his father while she headed back to their corner of the palace. She still felt dizzy and physically weak at the merciful reprieve from her worst possible fears. Jasim had become as precious to her as Sami and she was still in shock from the fright she had had. Ruefully conscious that stress and heat had left her clothing sticking to her damp skin, she went straight upstairs for a quick shower.

She was wearing only a bra and pants when she heard

Jasim return. Snatching up her wrap, she pulled it on and hurriedly knotted the sash before leaving the room to greet him.

'I'm sorry I was so long,' he groaned, 'But my father had a great deal to say to me—'

'I thought he might,' Elinor confided, hauling him closer with two possessive hands, drinking in the familiar musky scent of his skin and the rich honeyed aroma of the frankincense smoke that the staff were always wafting ritually over him. 'He was very upset. That's why I left you alone.'

'I am married to an angel of tact and intelligence,' Jasim drawled softly, holding her back from him to gaze down at her flushed and anxious face with unashamed appreciation.

'What happened to your cell phone this afternoon?'

'I was in such a frantic hurry to follow you back to Muscar that I left my phone behind at the villa.'

Elinor frowned. 'Why were you in such a hurry?'

'I knew I had to offer you a grovelling apology for ever having believed that you would lie to me.'

Her brows pleated. 'What are you talking about?'

Jasim dropped an arm round her slim shoulders and walked her into the bedroom. He dug into his shirt pocket and removed a photo and a sheet of paper. He gave her the photo first. 'I believe that this woman may be your mother, Rose.'

Elinor stared down in surprise at the photograph, which she had never seen before. It depicted her late mother with a much younger and slimmer Prince Murad, both of them clad in evening dress. 'Yes, it is. Where did you get it from?'

'It fell out of a copy of the Koran that Murad cherished…along with this letter.' He passed her the letter.

It was a letter written by her mother to Murad, telling him gently that they had to get on with their lives since they could not be together and that staying in contact would only make that more difficult. 'It's very sad,' Elinor whispered.

'Murad must have loved her very much to keep the photo and the letter for so many years. When I saw the date I understood why my brother did not ask for his father's permission to marry your mother. It was the same year that my mother deserted my father and clearly Murad saw no point in requesting the King's blessing for his marriage with a foreigner. My father was so bitter over what he saw as his own mistake that he would have refused. I'm afraid that if my brother told your mother that he was threatened with disinheritance, he was lying.'

Elinor was shaking her head in rueful comprehension. 'It's awful how something one person does can affect so many other lives in different ways.'

'But I misjudged you and insulted you,' Jasim reminded her darkly, brilliant dark golden eyes welded to her. 'I believed Yaminah's melodramatic suspicions and I kept on crediting her take on your relationship with Murad, even after I should have accepted that you were telling me the truth!'

'Yes, but you do tend to see wheels within wheels where none exist. You're jealous and possessive by nature,' Elinor pointed out ruefully. 'You make everything complicated—'

'No, I don't.' Jasim gave her a look of reproach.

'Well, you have since I met you. You always seem to expect the worst from women—'

'Yet I have received only the *best* from you,' Jasim interrupted, closing lean hands over hers. 'You are everything that I ever dreamt of finding in a woman. I know that now yet I almost lost you for ever. I feel sick at the thought that I might never have found you and Sami again.'

'You're hurting my hands,' Elinor told him apologetically. It did seem a very prosaic comment to make in the midst of that emotional flood of appreciation.

He lifted her crushed fingers to his lips and kissed them, massaging them to restore her circulation after the ferocity of his grip. 'It took me a long time to realise that I loved you. I didn't think I *could* fall in love and then I was too slow to recognise it when I did.'

Bemused by that declaration, she stared at him, scarcely daring to believe that he could mean what he was saying. 'I never thought I'd hear you say those words.'

'Neither did I,' Jasim confided, gathering her close to his lean, powerful frame. 'But I love you very much and I feel amazingly lucky to have you, *hayati*—'

'I love you too.' Elinor allowed her fingertips to trace one hard, angular cheekbone in a tender caress. 'I honestly believed that you were never going to feel the same way.'

'You must have suspected when I took you out to see the wild flowers,' he breathed in wonderment. 'I've never done anything like that in my life before with a woman.'

'I must have been slow on the uptake as well. I simply thought that you were trying to teach me about Quaram.'

'I believe I fell for you the first time I saw you on a horse.' His irreverent grin slashed his lean, strong face. 'You looked like a wild warrior woman: sexy, strong—'

Highly amused, Elinor smiled up at him. 'Whatever turns you on.'

'Unfortunately, my jealousy of the bond I believed you had already formed with Murad coloured everything,' Jasim admitted flatly. 'It clouded my reasoning. I couldn't wait to take you to bed because only then would you be really mine.'

Elinor linked her hands round his neck, loving the fact that he was just so basic and masculine in his reactions. 'Everything with you happened way too fast for me and I don't adapt well to things like that,' she murmured. 'We barely had five minutes together as a couple before I discovered that I was pregnant, and then playing a leading role in a shotgun marriage didn't make me feel any better about myself or the decision I was making.'

'I should have explained to you how I felt about marrying you behind my father's back. But I should also have looked to the future and made it a more joyful day.' Jasim frowned. 'I can see how my attitude gave you the impression that I was a reluctant husband and contributed to your lack of faith in me later that day when you overheard Yaminah.'

'It was just the last straw, but you weren't the only one of us who got it wrong. I should have confronted you, rather than just walk out.'

Jasim held her fast to him and tugged up her chin so that their eyes met. 'The worst of your sins was failing to get in touch even to tell me that you were well and safe. You were pregnant. I was afraid that you might have decided not to continue with the pregnancy.'

Her eyes widened in consternation. 'Jasim, *no*, I wouldn't have done that.'

'But I didn't know that,' he reminded her ruefully.

'I'm sorry I didn't phone you. I was horribly bitter. For a long time I thought I h-hated you.' Her voice faltering to a halt, Elinor wrinkled her nose. Her eyes were prickling with tears, the weight of stress she had borne earlier taking its toll on her, and she buried her face in his shoulder, needing the warmth and security of his closeness. 'But I think I still loved you and only hated you for hurting me.'

'I'll never hurt you again,' Jasim swore huskily. 'We have found so much together. I could not bear to lose it.'

'I was scared you would try to take Sami away from me when you found me again,' she confessed.

'I grew up without a mother and I would not have sentenced Sami to the same experience. But I was ready to put on the pressure, pull him away a little and make a lot of noise if it meant that you followed him and came back to Quaram with me.' Dark golden eyes vibrant with amusement as he made that frank admission, Jasim looked so gorgeous he made her mouth run dry. 'I wanted *both* of you back in my life full-time. For the eighteen months you were missing, you were all I thought about and other women didn't exist for me, *hayati*.'

'I wish I'd known,' Elinor lamented.

'Maybe I needed to lose you to fully appreciate you.' Tiring of talk, Jasim captured her mouth in an intoxicating kiss and her world went into a sensual spin. Gathering her yielding body into his arms, he urged her down on the bed.

The lingering edge of fear from the afternoon made her as eager for him as he was for her. They shed their garments in a tangled heap and rolled across the mattress welded to each other like magnets. But the act they shared was slow and sweet and joyful with love and mutual appreciation. Afterwards she lay replete and content and very weary in his arms, revelling in the tenderness in his eyes and the way he kept on telling her how much he loved her, words she knew she would never tire of hearing.

'Some day I'd like another child,' Jasim murmured

huskily, one hand splayed across her flat stomach. 'I would be there right from the beginning and I would not leave your side until the baby was born, *habibti*.'

Elinor was almost asleep, a dreamy smile on her lips. 'Some day, I might take you up on that,' she whispered.

Almost three years later, Elinor entered the nursery at Woodrow Court wearing a beautiful green satin evening gown and a magnificent set of emerald and diamond jewellery that glittered fierily below the lights.

Sami was tucked up in bed clutching a toy racing car. His sister, Mariyah, a dark-eyed toddler with her mother's ready smile, was fast asleep, and the newest addition to the family, Tarif, at four months old, was mesmerised watching the cot mobile above him with big drowsy eyes as it turned and played a lullaby. He was a laid-back good-natured baby who only cried when he was hungry. She was the mother of three children, Elinor reflected in bemusement, still amazed by the speed with which her life had changed and flourished. Mariyah, if truth be known, had not been planned, but the pregnancy had been easy and the delivery quick and Elinor had decided she would like her third child to be born within the same age range as the other two.

It was their fourth wedding anniversary and Elinor was content to look back on the three wonderful years she had shared with Jasim. They were rarely apart for, as his father's heir, Jasim travelled a great deal less. King Akil had outlived all the gloomy forecasts and, although he was by no means a well man, he had regained his appetite and a little weight and was certainly looking a good deal better. Jasim and his father often worked together now and had grown a great deal closer and that improved relationship had brought Jasim peace after his turbulent, unhappy childhood.

Elinor too led a very busy life. She had been asked to open the new hotel and leisure complex in Muscar. Soon afterwards she had agreed to help raise funds for a charity for premature babies, an interest that had led to countless hospital visits and other requests for her support. When Jasim was so much in demand she felt it was important that she had her own concerns and, between those and her desire to spend as much time as possible with her children while they were still so young, her daily schedule was pretty packed. Whenever she was in England she met up with Alissa and Lindy and she loved escaping the pomp and ceremony of life in Quaram to be treated just as a friend.

How had she dealt with Laila? Elinor's eyes sparkled at the recollection. She had leant on Jasim to issue invitations to palace functions to every eligible man he knew and, before very long, romance had worked its magic and Laila had been married and swept off to Oman by a very rich and besotted sheikh. Elinor got on very well with Laila's mother, Mouna, who looked on her as an extra daughter and adored the children.

Elinor had seen very little of her father in recent years but that was only what she had expected. Ernest Tempest had little interest in his grandchildren, and once he had satisfied his curiosity about the ancient history of Quaram further visits had had little appeal for the older man. Elinor believed she had already received more warm appreciation and encouragement from Jasim's father than she had ever received from her own.

At the King's instigation, the old rambling palace in the

desert outside the city had been renovated from top to bottom and the royal household had moved back there. Murad's monstrous noisy marble palace was now being used by the government as a conference centre, a parliamentary building and a museum. Yaminah had remarried and become stepmother to several children with her second husband. She had attended Jasim's birthday party the previous year. Elinor had enjoyed seeing Zahrah again and Yaminah had been scrupulously polite and pleasant as though all her wild suspicions had been laid in the grave with her first husband.

'What a picture you make,' Jasim breathed from the doorway.

In a whirl of fabric as her glamorous gown spun out round her, Elinor sped over to him. 'I thought you were going to be late—'

'For my anniversary dinner with my beautiful wife? Never!' Jasim teased, dark golden eyes smouldering with sensual appreciation over her before he curved an arm round her and walked round the nursery, bending down to say goodnight to Sami, laughing at the way Mariyah was curled up in one corner of her cot and smiling down at Tarif. 'But before we eat, I have something to show you. Unfortunately you're rather overdressed for our destination.'

'Shall I change?' Elinor asked.

'No, you look fabulous and I want to feast my eyes on you.'

'The emeralds are way over the top,' she sighed, her fingertips brushing the superb necklace.

'That was my father's gift,' he reminded her. 'And he doesn't do cheap or ordinary.'

She giggled like mad when he carried her out of the

house and stashed her in the Range Rover parked out front. 'Where on earth are we going?'

Jasim turned the car in the direction of the stables and she sat up straight, her level of interest growing, for the year before Jasim had given her a superb mare and she was a good deal more interested in horse flesh than she was in jewellery.

He helped her out and guided her over to the stables while she gathered her skirt up in one hand to stop it trailing. 'I have a surprise for you.'

'If it's got four legs, I'll love you for ever…well, I'll love you for ever whatever you do but more particularly if it's a live present.'

'Hush, *habibti*,' Jasim urged. 'She's been a little neglected and she's rather nervous, so the staff haven't subjected her to a decent grooming as yet.'

'Who?' Elinor was now nestling under his arm like a purring cat, for whenever he called her *habibti*, which meant 'beloved', she just melted inside.

A shaggy greyish-white head poked anxiously out over the stable door. The elderly animal in no way resembled the pedigree, perfectly groomed horses that usually occupied the boxes. Elinor stared at the homely mare with huge rounded eyes. *'Starlight?'* she whispered in disbelief, her voice cracking with emotion. She moved closer. 'My word, you've found Starlight for me! Is it any wonder that you're the love of my life?'

Jasim stood back watching while she petted the horse she had adored as a teenager and which her father had sold. He told her something of the mare's history since then and her eyes glistened with tears. After she had coaxed Starlight into trusting her again, she turned back to Jasim and flung herself at him in a passion of gratitude, hugging and kissing him with abandon.

'You really are wonderful,' she told him with shining eyes.

'You're the wonder in my life, *habibti*. I have you and I have three beautiful children, and I feel as though you have given me the whole world,' Jasim murmured huskily, studying her with quiet adoration.

Happiness bubbled up inside Elinor. 'I love you,' she whispered. 'And every day I'm with you, I love you a little more.'

* * * * *

"YOU HAVE MADE him proud," he told her, nodding at her
father, feeling benevolent. "You are the jewel of his kingdom."

Finally, she turned her head and met his gaze, her sea-
colored eyes were clear and grave as she regarded him.

"Some jewels are prized for their sentimental value,"
she said, her musical voice pitched low, but not low enough
to hide the faint tremor in it. "And others for their monetary
value."

"You are invaluable," he told her, assuming that would
be the end of it. Didn't women love such compliments?
He'd never bothered to give them before. But Gabrielle
shrugged, her mouth tightening.

"Who is to say what my father values?" she asked, her
light tone unconvincing. "I would be the last to know."

"But I know," he said.

"Yes." Again, that grave, sea-green gaze. "I am invaluable, a jewel without price." She looked away. "And yet,
somehow, contracts were drawn up, a price agreed upon
and here we are."

There was the taint of bitterness to her words then. Luc
frowned. He should not have indulged her—he regretted
the impulse. This was what happened when emotions were
given reign.

"Tell me, princess," he said, leaning close, enjoying the way her eyes widened, though she did not back away from him. He liked her show of courage, but he wanted to make his point perfectly clear. "What was your expectation? Do not speak to me of contracts and prices in this way, as if you are the victim of some subterfuge," he ordered her, harshly. "You insult us both."

Her gaze flew to his, and he read the crackling temper there. It intrigued him as much as it annoyed him—but either way he could not allow it. There could be no rebellion, no bitterness, no intrigue in this marriage. There could only be his will and her surrender.

He remembered where they were only because the band chose that moment to begin playing. He sat back in his chair, away from her. *She is not merely a business acquisition,* he told himself, once more grappling with the urge to protect her—safeguard her. *She is not a hotel, or a company.*

She was his wife. He could allow her more leeway than he would allow the other things he controlled. At least today.

"No more of this," he said, rising to his feet. She looked at him warily. He extended his hand to her and smiled. He could be charming if he chose. "I believe it is time for me to dance with my wife."

Indulge yourself with this passionate love story that starts out as a royal marriage of convenience, and look out for more dramatic books from Caitlin Crews and Harlequin Presents in 2010!

Sold, bought, bargained for or bartered

He'll take his…

Bride on Approval

Whether there's a debt to be paid,
a will to be obeyed or a business
to be saved…she has no choice
but to say, "I do"!

PURE PRINCESS, BARTERED BRIDE
by *Caitlin Crews*
#2894

Available February 2010!

PREGNANT BRIDES

*Inexperienced and expecting,
they're forced to marry!*

Bestselling Harlequin Presents author

Lynne Graham

brings you the second story
in this exciting new trilogy:

RUTHLESS MAGNATE, CONVENIENT WIFE
#2892
Available February 2010

Also look for

GREEK TYCOON, INEXPERIENCED MISTRESS
#2900
Available March 2010

TWO CROWNS, TWO ISLANDS, ONE LEGACY

*A royal family torn apart by pride and its lust for
power, reunited by purity and passion*

Harlequin Presents is proud to bring you the
final installment from The Royal House of Karedes.
As the stories unfold, secrets and sins from the past
are revealed and desire, love and passion war
with royal duty!

Look for:

THE DESERT KING'S HOUSEKEEPER BRIDE

#2891

*by Carol Marinelli
February 2010*

www.eHarlequin.com

HPI2891

REQUEST YOUR FREE BOOKS!

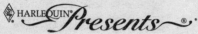

2 FREE NOVELS PLUS 2
FREE GIFTS!

YES! Please send me 2 FREE Harlequin Presents® novels and my 2 FREE gifts (gifts are worth about $10). After receiving them, if I don't wish to receive any more books, I can return the shipping statement marked "cancel". If I don't cancel, I will receive 6 brand-new novels every month and be billed just $4.05 per book in the U.S. or $4.74 per book in Canada. That's a savings of close to 15% off the cover price! It's quite a bargain! Shipping and handling is just 50¢ per book*. I understand that accepting the 2 free books and gifts places me under no obligation to buy anything. I can always return a shipment and cancel at any time. Even if I never buy another book, the two free books and gifts are mine to keep forever.

106 HDN EYRQ   306 HDN EYR2

Name	(PLEASE PRINT)	
Address		Apt. #
City	State/Prov.	Zip/Postal Code

Signature (if under 18, a parent or guardian must sign)

Mail to the **Harlequin Reader Service:**

IN U.S.A.: P.O. Box 1867, Buffalo, NY 14240-1867
IN CANADA: P.O. Box 609, Fort Erie, Ontario L2A 5X3

Not valid to current subscribers of Harlequin Presents books.

Are you a current subscriber of Harlequin Presents books and want to receive the larger-print edition? Call 1-800-873-8635 today!

* Terms and prices subject to change without notice. Prices do not include applicable taxes. Sales tax applicable in N.Y. Canadian residents will be charged applicable provincial taxes and GST. Offer not valid in Quebec. This offer is limited to one order per household. All orders subject to approval. Credit or debit balances in a customer's account(s) may be offset by any other outstanding balance owed by or to the customer. Please allow 4 to 6 weeks for delivery. Offer available while quantities last.

Your Privacy: Harlequin Books is committed to protecting your privacy. Our Privacy Policy is available online at www.eHarlequin.com or upon request from the Reader Service. From time to time we make our lists of customers available to reputable third parties who may have a product or service of interest to you. If you would prefer we not share your name and address, please check here. ☐

HP09R

HARLEQUIN *Presents*

EXTRA

**Presents Extra brings you
two new exciting collections!**

LATIN LOVERS

They speak the language of passion!

The Venadicci Marriage Vengeance #89
by MELANIE MILBURNE

The Multi-Millionaire's Virgin Mistress #90
by CATHY WILLIAMS

GREEK HUSBANDS

Saying "I do" is just the beginning!

The Greek Tycoon's Reluctant Bride #91
by KATE HEWITT

Proud Greek, Ruthless Revenge #92
by CHANTELLE SHAW

Available February 2010

I ♥ HARLEQUIN® *Presents*~

BROUGHT TO YOU BY FANS OF
HARLEQUIN PRESENTS.

We are its editors and authors
and biggest fans—and we'd
love to hear from YOU!

Subscribe today to our online blog at
www.iheartpresents.com